Roses for Meredith

CATHLEEN ELLIS

ISBN: 978-1-62967-063-8
Library of Congress Control Number: 2016901706

TO JOHN, WITH ME EVERY STEP...

OTHER BOOKS BY CATHLEEN ELLIS

www.CathleenEllis.com

A Scarf of Promise

Castle in the Air

Making Our Way

Kara's Love

Baskets on Christmas Lane

Up To Me

Christmas Bright

A Voice for Gabby

Love Ties

1

February 1988

"Studied long enough," she spoke out as she assembled her textbooks into her backpack.

She found her way among the crowds of students who exited the library. It was time for dinner, and she heard her tummy rumble in complaint. Meredith forgot to bring her usual trail mix for her study time. She stopped at her dorm front desk after she looked in her mailbox. The message said to stop at the front desk.

"Wow, you are one special little lady," the student assistant smiled to her as she brought out two vases. Each vase held a bright red rosebud with greenery surrounding the pert bud. Meredith looked at the small envelope attached to each vase. Each envelope had her name, Meredith Raymer, written on it. And she saw that the cards were from two different flower shops in Manhattan.

"Gosh, thanks for the message telling me they were here," she smiled to the assistant.

"Happy Valentine's Day, Meredith," the student assistant smiled back to her as she spoke.

"To you, also, Happy Valentine's Day."

Meredith unlocked her dorm room and brought in the roses. She placed them at her desk and unpacked her backpack, lining up her homework tasks for the evening.

She never studied in her dorm room; at night she studied in the dorm dining hall. It was not always quiet there, but she liked the openness of the big room and the bright lights. She never did study alone or in a computer lab.

"I'll wait to see who you guys are from; I got ta eat," she spoke to the roses.

Meredith found her roommate, Jennifer, at a table. Jennifer saved her a chair in the big dining hall.

"How was your day?" Jennifer asked.

"Busy, yours?"

"Same."

Meredith ate at breakneck speed, only half listening to the conversation around her.

"Got to get back to my room; stuff to do."

"See ya."

ॐ

Meredith held the cards and sat on her bed, propping her pillows behind her. She opened the first card.

"I miss you so much. I love you Meredith. I think of you. God bless and keep you. Happy Valentine's Day. Cole"

Meredith leaned over to her desk and picked up the vase from Cole. She smelled the rose, a hint of spice in its odor.

"Dear, dear Cole, will you never let me go?"

Meredith's mind spun back. Cole asked her out when she was 15. He was older. He went away to Iowa State, but returned to the family farm outside Porttown, Iowa, after three semesters. His dad got sick; Cole took over the farm so his younger brother could finish his degree at State. Then his brother returned to help him with the farm operation. After Cole came back to the farm, he tried to rekindle what he thought was a high school romance with Meredith. He told her several times before Meredith went to Kansas State that he wanted to marry her.

"Dude, not what I want; I'm going away to K State," Meredith shook her head and tried not to sound too happy as they faced each other at Christmas.

"How?" Cole looked into her defiant face, her stony eyes, "You'll turn 16 after Christmas."

"Right, and I've graduated from Porttown High, early, actually had enough credits at the end of last spring. But my folks, they wanted me to wait and start college at 16; don't think they realized that I am plenty mature to handle university life, and I can tell you for sure I can do the work."

"You've been busy while I was away at Iowa State."

"Yeah, I took enough AP classes to make me a second semester freshman. I start at K State next week."

"I knew you were a really smart kid; you just never talked much about your classes."

Meredith's mind rushed off as she looked at him. Then she thought, "That's because women who are pretty and have good minds must decide, let the home town guy know about smart, or let the guy want me for how good I look on his arm."

She recalled that as she smiled to Cole at that Christmas encounter with him.

ℰℴ

Meredith sat on her bed and put Cole's card down.

"That's enough, Cole, thanks for the rose; I'll call you to thank you. I need to be considerate of you. It hurts not to get what you want; I like pretty much have always gotten what I want," she spoke out.

Meredith opened up the second card.

"Happy Valentine's Day; you are special to me, Meredith. Love, Tyler."

Tears formed in Meredith's eyes as she took the card and held it to her breast.

"Oh, Tyler, your rose makes me very happy; you are special to me, too," Meredith whispered as her thoughts went to him. She held his rose in its vase as her mind brought up his image.

ଛ

She talked to her parents that weekend. It was their agreed upon time, Sunday afternoon.

"Thank you for my Valentine's card, and Conner, thanks for yours."

Her folks put on the speaker phone so all three of them could talk to her.

"Valentine's Day afternoon I got a big surprise."

"Tell us," her brother, Conner, urged her.

"A red rose from one young man, and another red rose from another young man."

"Cole?" her dad asked.

"Yes."

"And the other, if it's OK to ask?"

"Sure, from Tyler, he's civil engineering here, and a cadet in the Air Force ROTC program."

Meredith's mom spoke, "Two different young men, that's so nice Meredith, you are special to other people besides your family, your dad, me, and Conner."

"I guess I am, Mom."

"We love you, Meredith," they all said together as the phone conversation ended.

ଛ

Meredith registered for 18 credits her first semester at K State. She wanted to get a degree in Chemistry and to commission as an officer in the United States Air Force.

She liked her classes, especially chemistry, but ROTC caught her attention. She wanted a job when she graduated; she knew jobs might be hard to come by if there was a downturn in the economy. Her dad and many others predicted that event. Meredith would have a job if she commissioned as a 2nd lieutenant. With her degree in chemistry she foresaw she would end up in a Research and Development program with the Air Force or in a Defense program of some kind.

"I'm a lab rat," she told people who asked her why she chose chemistry as a major, "I'll help discover something that'll help mankind."

"I love working in chem lab, and I like morning physical training in my Air Force class," she said to her parents early on at the university.

"Yeah, Meredith, we remember your crazy chemistry experiments out in your little lab in the barn, from the time you started school," her mom reminded her.

"Uh huh, a couple times I tried to burn the whole place down."

Her parents chuckled, and Meredith joined in.

"Remember Richard Myers?"

"Not sure, help us Meredith."

"He's my hero; I got interested in ROTC. Hey he's from my detachment."

"That's right, you told us that."

"Yup, Tyler uses him as his model of an Air Force officer. Like Tyler, Richard Myers studied engineering at K State and also loved to fly, so he was a pilot, like Tyler wants to be."

"That awesome, Meredith, an Air Force officer as your hero," her dad cheered her.

ℂ

She and her parents continued to talk together on Sunday afternoons. Once in a while Meredith wrote them and they wrote back.

"We still like to hear the sound of your voice, and Conner is here to talk too," her parents told her each time they chatted on the phone.

∽

Meredith urged on the other women in Air Force ROTC Detachment 270. Twice a week the men and women of the detachment met at 0600 for physical training in a nearby gym on campus. Her positive attitude and her love of running caught the attention of the few other women in the detachment of eighty. The sit ups and push ups didn't faze her. Being a farm kid and helping her dad all her life gave her a strong body.

"Come on ladies, you can do it," she would talk out to the women who were having trouble as they did the exercises. Some women needed to lose weight, but most still had problems with the number of push ups and sit ups they were expected to do. Meredith felt lucky to get fitted with her blue uniform after her first try at picking out her uniform. She had pride in wearing her uniform all day Thursday. Air Force ROTC Leadership Lab was held on Thursday afternoons. That was her favorite time of the week. In the Lab she learned she was a leader most of her life; she just did not realize it until her first semester at K State.

She met Tyler Calva at Leadership Lab. He was a junior; his goal, he wanted a pilot slot. But he was studying to be a civil engineer, just in case the flying didn't work out. He introduced himself to her at the end of the first Leadership Lab.

"My Aerospace Studies officer said I have to play catch up, read the material covered last fall semester and know it. Otherwise I won't really understand what's going on in the program."

"So, Meredith, have you read the material?" Tyler smiled to her, asking the question in a gentle tone.

"I have, but I realize when I'm in the Tuesday Aerospace Studies class I often don't understand what my officer is referencing. I really need someone to quiz me, make sure I understand what's going on and where I might fit into the Air Force."

"I would be happy to do that, where do you study at night?"

"In my dorm dining hall, I need a little noise and I like the bright lights."

"What about weekends?"

"At the library, weekdays too when I'm not in class. I don't know hardly anyone, but that's OK. I'll get to know cadets in the program, that's enough for now. I'm in chemistry; I love the field, but it's intense. I study a lot."

She smiled to Tyler, her eyes bright with interest in him. Tyler and Meredith began to study together on Monday and Wednesday evenings at her dorm dining hall. He never forgot the first time he saw her walking toward him in the dorm waiting area. When she wore her blue uniform, she pulled her hair back at the nape of her neck. He saw her at morning physical training; she had on the Air Force shapeless shorts and t-shirt. But that night she had on skinny belted jeans, boots, and a bright red long-sleeved shirt tucked in. Her dark hair curled below her shoulders and down her back.

He gasped, catching his breath, not sure who he was looking at.

"Meredith, uh, is that you?" he asked, in a halting tone.

"Yeah, Tyler, this is what the campus sees, blue jeans, long sleeved shirt, boots. I am and will always be a farm kid. But I love being a cadet and dressing in my uniform." She smiled to him as she looked him in the face, "You look happy, relaxed, how did the midterm go?"

"Hard, I done good," Tyler nodded, a wide smile spread across his face.

They studied together for two hours. Tyler heard her summary of back chapters of her Aerospace Studies textbook and asked her questions about material he knew she must understand. Then they talked.

"Do you have wheels here?"

"Yeah, but I hardly ever take my car anywhere. I drive to church on Sunday; two other girls on my floor attend with me. So my wheels will get me to and from Porttown, and that's what my parents wanted. They don't have time to cart me around."

"You look real young, Meredith, how old are you?"

"Turned 16 after Christmas," her honey-colored hazel eyes blazed into his brown eyes.

Tyler whistled and raised his eyebrows, "Dude, how'd you get out of high school so early?"

"My early school teachers passed me along; I whizzed through school, took lots of classes at Porttown High, every year, as much AP as they'd let me, I'm a second semester freshman credit-wise, K State says, because of my big load in high school."

"Where's Porttown?"

"Smack dab in the middle of Iowa, off Interstate 35 and aways off Highway 30," she smiled to him, "now about you."

"From Lawrence, sure as heck didn't want to go to KU. So here I am with two more years to go in CE. I love my program, doing a little bit in water, but will do whatever the Air Force wants me to do."

"Career Air Force?"

Tyler smiled to her, "Certainly hope so. I need to get out of Kansas and see the world. I hope to do just that in my career path."

"You seem pretty sure of yourself," Meredith complimented him, looking at his handsome face.

"I am, I have confidence, just like the confidence I see in you," his brown eyes sparked into hers.

Meredith could not decide about Tyler's swarthy look. His light brown skin, coal black hair and delicious chocolate eyes made her think of people from Central America. She asked him.

"My dad's parents came here from Costa Rica. My dad is darker skinned than me; my mom has blue eyes and reddish hair. So, yes, I have a Spanish sort of background."

"Speak Spanish?"

"Yes, I'm fluent."

"I took Chinese, can speak enough to get by on a conversational level. But the writing and reading, so, absolutely difficult, practice practice practice with that language. What got me interested were a couple of Chinese workers we had one year helping with the corn; never seen anyone work as hard as they did. They helped me with conversational Chinese, so I learned the intonations from a Chinese speaker."

Tyler watched Meredith arch her eyebrows and nod her head in emphasis.

"I want to go out with you, Meredith," she watched his face and his serious eyes and knew he meant what he said.

"I appreciate that, Tyler, but I have a work ethic that tells me, study hard, see how midterms go, then, maybe in April I could accept a date with you. I am stubborn, single-minded in my purpose, and I have worked so hard to get to this university. I will not jeopardize that for anything. What I prize most about myself is my initiative," she smiled to him, nodding her head.

ॐ

Tyler remained patient, and their studying together continued. She did not invite him to her room after their study sessions concluded; she remained in the dining hall, often studying past midnight. After a month Tyler realized how driven she was. They talked to each other for a short while after each study session. By early April Meredith began to open up about her life before the university.

"My parents, well, so young, Mom was 17 when Conner was born, Dad 18. So in love, they told me. But whew, 18 months to the day that Conner was born, I was born. They had their hands full. Dad took over the corn operation on his dad's place, with the help of my Uncle Milt. My grandparents, dad's folks, moved to town, health problems. They died, way young. My parents live on the farm, in the farmhouse dad grew up in, my home too.

So there they were, my folks, mom still a teenager, she and dad with two kids and a farm to run. Uncle Milt is border-line retarded, but learned the farm operation from my granddad and my dad. Uncle Milt lives in a one bedroom place in the back part of the barn. He comes in for meals, but otherwise he lives by himself. He has a proper driver's license. But he feels he doesn't fit except in the farm world. My mom's real good to him, and Uncle Milt loves her, always said she was the best and only woman in his world. It didn't seem to bother my dad."

"When Conner was born, he was diagnosed with Down Syndrome. His eyes, ears, flat face and bigger tongue, my folks could see it even before the doctor told them. Conner and I grew up pretty much as twins. He was the sweetest and most loving little boy in the whole world. We learned to walk and talk together. I love my brother with my whole heart," Meredith paused, and then she started to tear up.

Tyler put his arm around her shoulders as they sat at the table. Meredith turned her tear-stained face to his, "Thanks," she lifted her eyes to his and beamed to him.

"For my mom, life took a terrible toll on her, raising almost twins, Conner with special needs, a husband who spent all his time with his work, as farmer dads do, and a brother-in-law who needed special attention from time to time. Life did get better for mom when Conner went to kindergarten and I went to Pre-K. It gave her a break for a little while each day. Mom taught my brother and me life skills as soon as we could grasp them. We learned to cook, clean, do laundry, and help dad in the fields. I'm tall, always was, Dad blocked up the gas and brake pedals on an automatic transmission pickup. I drove around on the farm from the time I was eight, Conner on the passenger side. We worked our butts off."

Meredith stopped. Tyler urged her to go on.

"Mom was the serious one, dad light-hearted. As we got older, it became pretty clear to me that the farm life, well, it wasn't for her. She went to work in the Porttown flower shop when I was nine. She loved it there; mom and dad asked me to take over running our home, the cooking and stuff. Life kinda righted itself for a few years. Because of my work ethic I handled everything. I just got organized; Conner helped. School did a terrific job with him. He was so happy, at school in special education and at home. When a bully beat him up pretty good in middle school, the bully's punishment was to spend a weekend at our home, so he could find out just what kind of life Conner had, and how hard Conner worked. Conner found new respect; no one ever bullied him again, because now everyone knew just how hard he worked and how much intelligence he had, in spite of his disability. I buried myself in my schoolwork, but I swore I would get out of that farm-life situation just as soon as I could. And here I am, and loving every second."

"Wow," Tyler nodded to her, "that is quite a story."

"Guys?" he looked into her eyes.

Meredith nodded to him, "One special, Cole, he was way old for me; he went away to Iowa State, but had to take over the corn operation for his dad after he'd been away three semesters, so left school. He asked me to marry him."

"And?"

Meredith saw Tyler's eyes questioning her.

Meredith shook her head and looked into his eyes, "My honest answer was no way, my highest goal or wish was to come to University, out of state, away from my family. I got my wish."

She smiled broadly to him, nodding her head. Tyler watched her face tinge with color.

"My deal is much like yours; wanted to get away from Lawrence, the Air Force itch's been in my blood for a long time."

"Your dad taught you everything he knew about cars, right?"

"For sure he runs the best automotive repair shop in Lawrence; the crazy busiest place I ever was in. He's booked 10 days in advance, but saves time slots for emergencies."

"Did you help him?"

"Yeah, from the time I was 12 and tall enough to see down into the engine, I worked along side his other mechanics. But when I got my driver's license, I moved on to what I love the most, working on airplane engines for smaller planes. I'm torn, sometimes, between wanting to be an airplane mechanic and wanting to be a pilot."

"The money?"

"Yeah, Meredith," he nodded to her, "it's always the money. My dad makes a very good living, but my folks are frugal. Mom works part time at a coffee shop, does the books and helps waitress. They put everything away for college for me and my younger sister."

"Some of the cadets have their private pilot's license. Do you?"

"I do," Tyler smiled, "I moved from working on plane engines to flying the dang things, been jinormously expensive for the flying lessons, but dad wanted to do it for me."

He laughed, a swirl of memories attacked his head as he told her that.

"So I'm a lab rat and you're a plane jockey."

They laughed together at her comment.

"Maybe I could take you up in a plane I use; I have to keep flying and updating my flying hours."

Meredith gave him a quick smile, "I'll see, gosh we are busy students."

Tyler packed his books in his backpack. They held hands as she walked him to the dorm entrance.

He held her in a close hug. He moved away from her and put his hand on the side of her face.

"You are so special to me, Meredith."

"Back atcha, as you are to me."

She moved her lips to his. They stayed in the soft kiss until Meredith began to feel unsteady on her feet. She opened her eyes and moved her lips away from his.

They came into a hug again.

"It feels so good, with my arms around you, Meredith," he smiled into her darkened eyes.

She nodded and watched him exit through the glass doors. He looked back, and she waved to him.

&

The semester sped along. Chem Lab and Leadership Lab remained her favorite classes. Tyler asked her to be his partner at the Air Force ROTC Awards ceremony at a hotel in Manhattan. The dinner and awards part were fun. But what surprised Meredith the most was the DJ who provided music later in the evening. She loved dancing with Tyler. They spun and twirled around the dance floor set up in one section of the room where the Awards ceremony took place.

He drove her back to her dorm and walked her in to the front reception area.

"Awesome time, Tyler, it was totally awesome being with you. And congratulations again on your special scholarship to help you with your final time here. You all in engineering get some pretty special treatment."

Tyler smiled to her, "That's true, Air Force really wants engineers. And the engineering program here also takes good care of us. But Meredith, the Air Force'll want you, you'll be a scientist."

She gave him a hug and stepped back from him, "Our futures, so bright, so special."

Tyler nodded his head to her, "My firm hope, that's for sure."

He kissed her, and they parted with a squeeze of their hands.

&

"Sweet pea, how did finals go?"

"Awesome, it pays off to work hard every single day, to never slack off."

"Dad, you're calling me; I'm almost packed; I'll drive tomorrow, be home tomorrow night, why the call?"

"Honey," Meredith heard her dad's voice falter, and then she heard him start to cry. Meredith felt a crush in her throat and tears in her eyes. For a moment she did not utter a word.

"Dad, talk to me, tell me what in the world is going on."

"OK honey, I've pulled over to the side of the road, calling you from a gas station, near the farm. I've been to town."

"Dad, talk," Meredith said in a determined voice.

"I just saw a counselor, Meredith. We haven't talked for several weeks, remember, you went flying with Tyler one Sunday and then you were at the library cramming for finals."

"You're right, go on Dad, sorry, I sorta lost track of the weeks and the Sunday calls."

Meredith's hands sweat so bad she had to switch the phone to her other hand. She felt wet on her forehead.

"I didn't want to tell you, because your finals were very critical, but now I must, sweet pea."

"Tell me what?"

"A month ago your mom left us, me and Conner."

"What?" Meredith's voice whispered; she could not talk in a normal tone. She felt the bile rising up in her throat. She tried to swallow.

She choked it out, "Left you, left you for, well, where did she go?"

"She got in her car from work at the flower shop and drove to Santa Barbara, to live with your Aunt Sandra."

"Not!"

"Yeah, it's nuts, Meredith. That's why I'm seeing a counselor; Conner's going with me next time. Oh and the group-living home where Conner stayed closed down. He's been living back here on the farm. He was home two days when his mom walked away. He blames himself for her leaving. But, Meredith, your mom's been unhappy for a long, long time. She held it all together because you were such a huge help at the house, and on the farm, and with

Conner, and with Uncle Milt, and helping out at the flower shop. No one realized what an impact you had on us until you were gone for about 10 days. Honest to pete, young lady, how in the world did you do it all plus study and make great grades?"

"I learned it from you, Dad, super organized, a solid businessman, a knowledgeable farmer. You know your stuff, golly Iowa State uses some of your fields for test corn. You have a great relationship with the ag folks there. Dad, you're just top notch."

Jack Raymer paused, comprehending what his daughter just told him. "Thank you Meredith, for your wonderful compliment. Your mom stopped taking care of things here after you were gone for a month. I keep my business stuff in order, but the house, you really did everything there."

"Who drives Conner to work now that he doesn't live in town and ride his bike to the store?"

"Either I or Uncle Milt, or one of our help takes him, and he calls us to let us know when he needs to come home at the end of the day. Then I or Uncle Milt go get him. He's been working 10 and 11 hour days at the grocery store. And his days changed. He gets Monday and Tuesday off at the store, so he helps me on the farm on those days. I do make him take time off to rest because he works so hard. He's the saddest I've ever seen him. And he's such a happy kid. What he says now is that his work and helping me is his whole life. I hope another group home may start up, and Conner could live there. He did just great at the home."

"Dad, he's self-sufficient. He works more than a 40 hour week, has a banking account, a state id, and a certificate of attendance from Porttown High. I know he'll never qualify for a driver's license; he knows that too. He's learned to get around really well on his bicycle. But it's too far for him to ride his bike from work to home. Someday he'll be able to get his own place."

"Meredith, I am asking you to come home. I know you just planned to stay a week and head back to summer school there. Honey, the shit just keeps piling higher and higher."

"I got it, Dad, and of course I'll come home. My family comes first."

"Thanks, Meredith."

"Oh, honey, I kinda went crazy a few days ago. I got it in my head to do updating in the house. Your mom updated the kitchen: the appliances, the sink, new cupboard fronts and counter tops. Back when we pulled up the kitchen carpet we found wood flooring underneath, you'll remember, found out that wood went throughout the house, from a long time ago. Anyway Milt, Conner and me, we stripped off that awful wallpaper in the living room and hallway and painted the walls off-white. Then we ripped out all the carpeting and pad in the dining room, living room and hallway. Floor people are redoing the floors. We hope to have everything done for when you get home. Oh, there's a blue dumpster to the side of the garage, for one last big trash dump."

"Dad, if doing the fix up makes you feel better, then it was a good thing."

"It does make me feel better. I think you'll be pleased. Be safe and we'll see you soon."

∞

"Tyler."

"Meredith, are you OK? We agreed to talk next weekend after you get back for summer school."

Meredith burst into tears and cried and cried into her phone.

Tyler held his phone and waited for her to calm down.

"Babe, tell me."

Meredith explained her situation, what her dad told her.

"It might not make much sense, but that's what's happened, Tyler."

"I am so so sorry, Meredith. I had a friend, a girl, at my high school; her dad did the same thing, walked out on the family. What can I do to help?"

"Pray, pray to God for me and for my family. Pray for my mom; I think she needed to do this walk away years ago; from what dad says I was the glue that sorta held the family together. But once I was gone I think mom lost hope and saw that greener pastures somewhere else were all she had left to look forward to. Yeah, I've heard of this happening; I wonder how many other worked-to-death farm wives would do what mom did if they had the chance. Dad loves what he does, and he's had a very good life, so have I, until now. Really, this is the first big disappointment of my life. I'm not handling it well."

"Tell me Meredith, how do you feel about all this?"

"Sucks, mad as hell, sad, I worked so hard to get away from that place. I'm absolutely spoiled. Now my dad is asking me to come back."

"You'll do it, you'll help him?" Tyler asked in a soft voice.

"Of course, he's my dad."

"Meredith, you're 16, but way more mature than your age. My dad is an auto mechanic, but somewhere he shared with me a farm image, and he's repeated it to me several times over the years."

"What's that, Tyler?"

"Dad looks at me with his big brown, very solemn eyes and says, 'Grow where you're planted.' I used to not understand that, but now I do."

"Thanks Tyler, I'll remember your dad's phrase, I know it will help me as I struggle to understand why this is happening to me."

"Meredith, not why, but what are you going to do now?"

"Yeah, right, I'm going to drive home, help my dad, brother and uncle; the flower shop needs me too. I know the owner was ready to turn the daily operation completely over to mom."

"That sounds good, Meredith, that plan sounds good."

"I'll miss you, Tyler."

"Hey, I can fly to an airport around Porttown and see you."

"That's right, oh yeah you're headed to AFROTC Summer Camp, right, to be a cadet leader. It'll be great; our detachment Colonel is running this camp."

"You remembered, but it won't be all summer, just four weeks, starting next week. We'll see each other, I promise. God bless and keep you, Meredith. He'll watch over you as He watches over me."

"Actually, I been cursing God a little bit; gotta cut that crap out. I know He loves me, has me in the circle of His arms, but right now I'm beating God on His chest. I'm just so angry, in the way I talk to Him."

Meredith paused. Tyler heard a big sigh from her, "He knows best; it's His will for me."

"Hope you can accept that, Meredith."

"Tyler, I'm in His loving arms."

"Good for you; take care; we'll talk after camp is over."

"Take care, Tyler, I know you'll do great with the cadets at camp. I see you as such a leader, God bless you."

2

"Need to start looking at what is smack in front of me, instead of projecting ahead so far. I can be grateful and happy, here and now, with all that I have. I must cherish my life, and enjoy each day. I will not be studying every minute of every hour of every day. Maybe, God, are you trying to tell me something by having this happen to me?"

Meredith asked that question out loud to God all the way from Manhattan to Porttown. She beat her hands on the steering wheel until they were sore. She cried, she sang, she recited the Table of Elements, even put a song to it, something she'd heard from an old-time comedian. She talked out some of her chemistry equations. She drove down the road to her farm home, looking from side to side at the fields. Meredith saw the corn, just peeking green leaves out of the ground. She remembered her dad telling her that they planted starting on April 20, planting all done for now.

Meredith nodded her head, "I know now how he had time to work on the house inside, plantin' over. Oh, the trees are so beautiful, so leafed out nice. Everything looks fresh and clean," she said to herself.

"Dad, you do a bang up job with outside appearances. As always things are neat and painted and up to snuff,"

Meredith spoke out as she parked in the driveway and headed up the walk to her front door.

The locked door made her aware that no one might be home. She found her house key on her key ring and let herself in. Meredith breathed in deep; as she exhaled she looked all around her. The smell hit her nose, causing her to choke and cough. Her home smelled of freshly varnished wood. The living room looked big. The familiar furniture seemed smaller to her. She looked at the fresh painted walls; the wallpaper was gone, like dad said. Meredith knelt down and touched the wood floor.

"Wow, this is so beautiful," she spoke out as she admired the old wood, now revitalized with a beautiful dark tan stain with varnish over that. "This won't show the dust from outside so bad, good job, dad," she said.

Her home was small, but it appeared larger to her now as her eyes took in the same color paint and same flooring throughout the main area. She saw a note on the kitchen counter.

Welcome home Meredith. Gone to town to pick up Conner from work. We'll have pizza for dinner. It's in the freezer. Don't worry about the windows and French door with no window coverings. New stuff will be coming on Monday, installed too. Like the new look? Love Dad P.S. Garage a mess, can't put your car in it. Ditto for laundry room.

Meredith walked through her home. She opened the door to her bedroom. Happy tears came to her eyes as she looked around at the few things she kept out before she left, books, her French horn in its case, her whole previous life. She saw a small vase of flowers on her desk. Meredith looked at the note under the vase.

It was Conner's careful printing, I'M SO HAPPY MEREDITH. YOU ARE HOME AND I LOVE YOU. Conner

She held the note in her hand. She looked up and around at the light peach coloring of her room.

"Meredith, get a grip," she spoke out, "people love you, maintain a positive attitude about all this. Look at what dad and Conner and Uncle Milt are capable of. Think of this fix up as something for me. It needed to be done. We all have to move on with our lives. Know this, if mom and dad don't work this out, there may be someone else come into each of their lives. Love is still out there."

Meredith's tears came now; she knew at that instant that her life made a big change. She got down on her knees, held her hands in prayer and leaned into her bed.

"God, help me not to fight this change, help me grow where I'm planted," she cried.

She took her hands and wiped away the tears streaming down her face. With deliberate steps she began bringing in her belongings from school. She took everything straight to her room and began to make order.

"I better look in the garage, to see what dad meant," she said as she opened up the door to the garage. She looked around, and her stomach started flopping.

"This is a disaster; it stinks," she shouted, "here I go again, the cleanup man."

She stepped back into the house and closed the door. She counted to ten, then to 100. It worked; she calmed down. She took deep breaths, in and out, in and out. Meredith looked around at the neat kitchen. Her dad and Conner kept it clean and uncluttered; Meredith insisted they rinse out their dishes and put them in the dishwasher. The habit took; they still did what Meredith asked them to do from the time she was 12. She peeked in the freezer.

"Yeah, the pizzas; I'll cook both 'cause Uncle Milt likes pizza too."

Outside she noticed that it began to get dark. Meredith started the pizzas. Soon her dad and Conner arrived home. After they all ate, Meredith sat in amazement as the big smiles remained on their faces, on Uncle Milt's too.

"You guys seem like you really missed me. That makes me feel good. To be honest I didn't have time to think about home."

"Mere, (mare) did you ever get homesick?" Conner asked her as he helped her clean up the dishes.

"Only on Sundays, at church, and when I talked to you and mom and dad on the phone. That's all, Conner. Studying took all my time."

Conner put his hand on her upper arm. "Mere, I missed you very much. But I know you will go back to school, once dad and mom figure out about their lives. Going to counseling with dad. We lost someone we care about, mom."

Conner stood five inches shorter than Meredith. Meredith looked down to see the tears in his blue eyes. She stopped what she was doing and gathered him in her arms. He put his arms around her.

"That feels so good; hugs are so good. Thank you, Mere. I love you," he said to her as they stayed in the hug.

"Thank you for the flowers and the note, Conner. That was very thoughtful of you."

"I asked dad about doing that; he said it was a very good idea."

Conner had work tomorrow so he went off to bed. Meredith and her dad sat at the dining room table and talked between loads of washing and drying.

"I know, I know what your next question will be, yes I know you saw the dumpster, so we can clear the garage and put our vehicles back in."

"Dad, how did it get so bad out there?"

"Lazy, didn't take the time, so we just chucked stuff. Baby girl, the corn is planted, that's the very good news. Now, pray for rain and good weather, and nice crop conditions. I got pretty messed up for a few days after your mom left."

Meredith moved her eyes to her dad's. She watched as tears came to his eyes. She waited for what he had to say.

"I drank myself through a four-day binge. Milt asked me to straighten myself up; he'd never done that. He said I was only hurting myself and accomplished nothing except an enormous hangover. He's doing his best to help out. So now I restrict myself to a beer a night, but only if I'm not driving."

"Mom?"

"Yeah, she's OK, she called once, saying she got there and was looking for work. This is tough, but she asked that you kids not try to contact her for awhile. She emphasized to me to make sure and tell you that she loves you, always will, but it needs to be from afar for a while. She knows you and Conner are self-sufficient and will be fine. Meredith, she did an excellent job raising you two. I was just the guy you saw at night and on Sundays; I tried to keep that as a family day."

"Dad, I'll be going to church. I did back at school. If you want to, you and Conner can come with me," her eyes implored her dad's.

"Yes, I'll come tomorrow. Conner can't now because his days off are Monday and Tuesday. But his days off may change. He's doing a bang-up job at the grocery store. They are proud of him. He's fulfilling a goal of the store owner, to hire a mentally-challenged person, to show the public that Conner is also a fine worker."

"So he bags groceries?"

"Yes, Meredith, that's one of his many tasks at the store. He also helps with deliveries, in the butcher shop, and with janitorial. I am proud of him, Meredith, just as I am proud of you, your grades are outstanding. You are such a hard worker."

Meredith watched her dad's eyes shine as he complimented her. She smiled to him.

"Thanks, Dad, I sure got that from you."

Jack touched his daughter's shoulder, "And from mom, too. She is very responsible for everything about this place, truly a teammate in our effort to have an effective farm operation and raise two fine kids."

ℰↄ

Uncle Milt drove Conner to work on Sunday so Jack and Meredith could attend church. The Raymers were members of First United Methodist Church in Porttown. Reverend made one main point in his sermon, and he kept the sermon short. Meredith liked that. And the choir sounded especially great that day. They shook hands with Reverend Hartman as he greeted them outside.

"Meredith, welcome back, I hope you will help the choir with your French horn playing from time to time. We enjoyed that so much," the reverend shook her hand and smiled to her and then to her dad.

"I'll contact the choir director when I get settled to see when I could help."

"The whole congregation loved your playing, thanks Meredith."

Jack Raymer greeted six couples as they walked from the church to their car.

Their standard response was, "We're all thinking of you, Jack, our prayers go out to you and your family."

They seemed happy to see Meredith and welcomed her back.

"Would you mind driving home, Meredith, I'm a little rattled, first time I've seen some of these folks in a while. I hadn't been to church since the Sunday after Valentine's Day. It felt good to be there today. And it would be great for you to play with the choir; you're an excellent horn player."

Meredith turned to him as they headed out of town. She saw the sadness in his eyes as he looked straight ahead.

"I'm glad, Dad, that you liked church today. I plan to attend church every week that I can. You're always welcome to come with me; it's up to you. I know stuff will get busy for you as the corn season progresses."

"My biggest problem now is my pride, my stupid ego. My counselor is helping me with that. There's a hole in my heart where love should go; I tried with your mom. I guess I failed."

"Dad, time, give it time, that's what all of us need as we adjust to what's happening to us day to day."

Her dad chuckled, "Sweet pea, how did you get so wise?"

He touched her shoulder as she turned into the lane toward their home.

"From you, my handsome and wise dad."

She flashed him a big smile with a tone of compliment in her voice.

"We're gonna be OK, kid," he said to her.

Meredith heard confidence in the timbre of his voice, like the fullness of a well-played cello.

She looked over to him as she parked.

"We ARE going to be OK," she smiled to him.

※

Meredith liked the food arrangement her dad had. Conner bought groceries they needed from the list the family gave him. He did the grocery shopping on Wednesdays and Sundays. So whoever picked Conner up from work those nights also got to bring home the groceries. Conner liked the task; he knew it helped his family to do a job that would ordinarily take several hours a week away from a busy farm. Because he worked in the butcher shop, he knew how to pick out meat. Meredith noticed the nice cuts of meat in their freezer. For her first Sunday dinner home, Meredith wanted to cook a pork roast with potatoes and gravy. She would make it her homecoming dinner for her three guys.

Meredith changed into shorts and a t-shirt after church and made quick sandwiches for her dad, Uncle Milt and her. She started in on the garage by opening the garage door and letting air into the fetid and decaying trash.

"You guys are a bunch of slobs," she cried after she spent 15 minutes separating trash.

"Do you want some help, Meredith?" she heard her dad ask as he passed by the garage.

"I got it, Dad. You never would allow a mess like this out in your precious barn."

She spat out the words, "precious barn."

Jack watched his daughter's face get redder and redder from her exertions.

"You're right; I would never do that to my barn. I am sorry."

"Dad, leave. Know that if I put it in the dumpster it's gone. When do they come and pick the dumpster up?"

"Tomorrow afternoon, it's our regular trash day, if you'll remember."

"So the dumpster will be gone for good."

"Right, Meredith, good, you're calming down a little, I've really upset you."

"Dad, you know how I want order and peace and quiet, that's the OCD (obsessive compulsive disorder) I get from you."

"Yeah, kid, you're your father's daughter, for sure."

"Enough, Dad, don't hover, leave me before I get upset again and start screaming."

"I'm gone," Jack raised his hands and smiled to her, knowing to get the hell away from her.

Meredith took a break and had a pop, something she rarely did. She tried to drink just water or milk or coffee, her favorite was coffee. She missed that at school; her dorm cafeteria never made enough coffee to suit her.

She hauled bag after bag of garbage over to the dumpster and heaved each bag in. She flattened all the boxes so they would take up the least amount of room in the dumpster.

"My shoulders are on fire," she spoke out as she grimaced from moving her shoulders. She dropped and did eight pushups, but could not do any more. "I got to start working out; I let my exercising slide studying for finals.

Now I can make order in here; what's left belongs in here," she spoke out to the garage.

A half hour later she met her goal. She moved her small car into the garage, on the right side. She left room for her dad's bigger pickup on the left. She heaved herself out of her car and thrust her keys into her shorts pocket.

"Meredith, oh Meredith, you're home. I'm so glad."

Meredith heard a sort of familiar voice and turned toward the open garage door. She stood there in disbelief.

Cole looked her over. He saw her red, steamy face, her ponytail loosening from its rubber band. Her t-shirt rimmed with sweat around the neck and in the curve between her breasts, and her shorts looked filthy. She wore dirty gloves.

"I love you, Meredith," he told himself, but did not speak out to her.

"Hi, Cole. You just missed being a part of the most miserable clean-up effort I've had in a while."

"Hey, I'm glad I missed that," he smiled as he spoke to her. "Conner told me in the store that you were back. It's good that you'll be helping your dad out. I am so sorry about your mom."

Meredith heard the sympathy in his voice.

"Dad says she's OK out in California, that's all we know. Mom doesn't want us to contact her; she'll get in touch with us when the time is right."

They stood in the sunshine. Everyone always said they were a picture-perfect couple. Cole stood 6'3", a blue-eyed blonde, muscular and buffed from working all his life on a farm. Meredith was 5'8", with dark hair and honey-colored eyes, and long legs. She was his first love. Cole knew he would never forget her, couldn't get her out of his mind, despite her being gone.

"Did you, did you, miss going through graduation from high school, and all the stuff that went along with that?"

She looked him in the eye, "Nah, not a bit, I was where I wanted to be, at K State, working in my beloved chemistry lab; I requested and got to do a couple of special experiments, just sewed up the A I was getting."

"I have news, Meredith."

"Tell me."

"I'm marrying Ginny Ann Mandrin."

"Thank God, thank you God," Meredith said to herself.

She smiled to Cole, "Congratulations, Cole; when's the big day?"

"A week from Thursday; she's over three months pregnant with our kid."

They hugged and stepped away from each other.

"Cole, I'll keep you in my thoughts and prayers, that's a big load you are going to saddle up too," her honey-colored eyes glittered into his.

"Uh huh, but I can handle it; just like when I took over the farm."

Meredith heard the confidence in the tone of his voice and his expression.

"Take care now," she smiled as she spoke to him.

She waved to him as he walked back to his pickup and looked back to her. He put on his sunglasses as he wheeled his pickup around and down the lane from the farm home to the road. He cried hard, big tears that threatened to blind him. He gulped for breath until he was on the highway for a while.

"Meredith isn't out of my life yet; I been holding Ginny Ann in my arms, but it's Meredith I love," he muttered as he clenched the steering wheel, white knuckles showing.

℅

"Wow, thank you Ginny Ann, whoever you are. You just made my life a whole lot simpler, taking care of Cole for me," Meredith shouted out as she washed her hands and arms and face at the kitchen sink.

She heated the oven and got the pork roast ready by adding a little red wine, potatoes, and onions to the roast in the pan. After that she showered and set the dining room table with the family's good dishes, left to them by her Grandma Raymer.

Uncle Milt, her dad and Conner laughed a lot at Meredith's homecoming dinner. They shared stories about each other, from their earlier days and experiences with each other. Conner's surprise was a cake. They all swore they could not eat another bite after dinner. But Conner cut into the cake anyway, and everybody had a piece of cake with ice cream.

"Wow Conner, it's carrot cake, your favorite," Meredith spoke to Conner.

"I remember how much you like dessert, Mere."

"Yeah, she has a huge sweet tooth," Uncle Milt chuckled and they all laughed.

"In that case, I'll cut one and one half pieces for myself," Meredith looked around as they continued to laugh.

"Me and my bro, we'll do clean up, Meredith. That was an outstanding meal. We really got pretty sick of store bought oven dinners, sweet pea."

Jack gave his daughter a big smile as they all helped clear the table.

ℰↃ

That night Meredith had trouble falling asleep.

"I'm sad; I feel bad for mom. I hope she finds work; I want her to have a good life. I've never wanted for anything. God guide her, and me," she prayed.

She dug out her chemistry book and did some review work. She awoke the next morning with the book by her side and her lamp still on.

ℰᴑ

"Dad, I feel like, well that I've been back here for a while. It's just a couple days."

She stood at the kitchen counter fixing her breakfast. Her dad was already at the table eating.

He looked across to her, "Meredith, you been mighty busy since you got home, your room set to rights, the garage all fixed up, the meals you've cooked for us. Today you're going in to meet with Phyllis and work the day, right?"

"Yeah, need to meet Phyllis at 9:30. She has someone opening up the shop. She wants to meet me at a nearby coffee shop to talk. Then we'll head into the shop. I spoke a few words to her; it's a crazy week, heck, month, really a whole summer of lots of work for the shop."

"The window treatment people are coming at 10:00. I think you'll like what they helped me decide to do. It'll be what they call an airy look. I don't get that lingo, but I think our home will look nicely updated. Conner is helping me with the window stuff, and then we have fields to check."

"Dad, did you use Imadaclopid-treated seeds this year?"

"Yup, me and State U. well, tried several different chemical treatments, but on the test fields we've found Imadaclopid has the best corn yield per bushel. So now I plant those chemically treated seeds on all the fields.

"What's your treatment?"

"1.34 mg/kernel."

"A big dose."

"Yeah but we have six different pests that want to eat the succulent kernels of my corn. So that's it, we've found the answer, at least for this season, we think."

He emphasized the words we think.

"Corn growing is a crap shoot, Dad," Meredith shook her head and looked into his eyes as she sat down with her coffee.

"Actually, Meredith, as you are well aware, it's all about the chemistry of knowing what works with what."

"It's why I'm studying chemistry, Dad. I must unlock the answers to problems, in farming, in industry, and for a while in defense, when I do become an Air Force officer."

Jack saw the determination in his daughter's serious eyes.

"It sure is good to have you home."

Meredith kissed his cheek as she got up and finished her coffee. After she put her coffee cup in the dishwasher, she felt a presence next to her leg. Meredith looked down.

"Jeepers, is that you?"

She knelt down and hugged the reddish-brown husky/collie she grew up with. Jeepers gave her a lick across her cheek.

"How's my old friend?" Meredith looked into Jeeper's deep brown eyes.

Milt stood nearby.

"He's got the arth-a-ri-tis real bad in his back legs. Mostly sits around my place, goes out only when he has to. But I told him Meredith was back, and he wanted to see you."

"Ah, thanks Uncle Milt; that's kind of you. Good boy, Jeepers. Maybe I can take him out for short walks; I'm told that helps a dog with arthritis to get exercise," she looked up at her Uncle Milt as she said that.

Milt smiled to Meredith, "He'd like that, a lot."

She nodded her head to him and gave Jeepers another hug.

ɮ

Meredith sat across from Phyllis at the café just down the street from the flower shop.

"I ain't gonna sugar coat this for you, Meredith. I'm in a terrible mess. I need you full time, some full Saturdays, Sundays off. Can I count on you?"

"I am so sorry mom left you in dire straits, Phyllis. Of course, I'll help out. The farm seems manageable, feels like I've not been gone."

Meredith took Phyllis's hand and squeezed it.

"Was plannin' to turn the whole shop over to your mom. It looked like that would work out. Your mom took some classes and is a certified wedding planner. She was going to handle six weddings, two per month for the next twelve weeks, basically through the summer. I am so sorry your mom was having problems; she never hinted that she was making other plans."

"Mom's stoic, didn't ever verbalize much, very serious. When she said something, which wasn't often, she meant it. So I can understand why she never spoke up to you. But it's not fair that she didn't give you two weeks notice."

"Has she been unhappy for a long time, Meredith, I know, it's none of my damn business?"

Meredith teared up as she looked at Phyllis, "Yes, I believe it's been for many years."

"Oh dear Lord, babe I'll keep your mom and all the Raymer family in my prayers; I swear on my old Bible that I did not know what was going on in her mind, so close-mouthed."

Meredith nodded. They each sipped their coffee.

Phyllis started to smile, "I complimented your mom on taking the correspondence wedding planner training. Maybe I have an idea why she did that, got her certification, might help her get employed where she's landed."

"Six weddings, whew," Meredith paused, casting a doubtful face to Phyllis. "Do you have kind of a manual on how that all will work out? And a calendar of what happens when?"

"I do have; your mom took bunches of notes from each bride. There's a notebook sectioned off by bride; she showed it to me, along with an individual timeline on each wedding event. Will you take over those six weddings for me, Meredith?"

"Wow, sounds like a huge challenge, yes I will try," Meredith's forehead knotted as she looked at Phyllis.

"Dena will help you; she worked with your mom on all the weddings your mom's done for the past nine months. So she knows the deal. The weddings are a money maker for the shop. Your mother negotiated for a cut of the wedding profit. I'll do the very same for you, and for Dena, a 50/50 split, since she will be leading out, at least for a while, 'til you get your feet wet."

"Mom, she always kept her word, trustworthy, she always followed through on things for me, the family. I guess she operated that way in the shop."

"She did, Meredith, we have a solid reputation in our community for great service, outstanding flowers and flower arrangements and happy customers. That's why other shops have come and gone in this town. We are the one and only, the best."

Phyllis smiled to her.

"Customer service, Phyllis, you've always demanded that. And it's paid off."

Phyllis nodded her head, "Big time."

Meredith asked her about her wages. She gave Phyllis an hourly amount. Without a moment's hesitation Phyllis agreed. Meredith committed to help through the end of the year, over six months until she returned to K State.

As Meredith walked down the street with Phyllis after their coffee, her mind swirled.

"Dad and mom should have something figured out by that time. I'm pretty sure I know the outcome right now, but God, you're in charge. God bless and keep my folks, and me."

&

By mid-afternoon of her first Monday at the shop Meredith's head spun. Phyllis showed Meredith the new calendar order system that a world-wide flower service established for the shop. Meredith also discussed the flower waste that she saw around her as she worked part time in the shop during her last two years of high school.

"Frankly, we're making a big effort to clean that up, being more careful, with our flowers, with our ordering. We have four deliveries coming in every week. Sometimes both our big coolers are jammed along with the display case out front when there's a big event," Phyllis nodded and smiled.

"Have you thought about having a volunteer take extra left-over flowers to our nursing home, and to our independent/assisted living facility?"

"Missy," Phyllis paused and smiled to Meredith, "oh, that's a fabulous idea, when we have waste. I'll let you lead out on that if you would. You may know gals who might be willing to do that once a week or so. It would be a great volunteer effort for a gal; you know, it could be a high school student, maybe a junior or senior who likes to work with flowers and has a car. Meredith, I really like the way your mind works. You're smart as a whip, gonna make a solid businesswoman," Phyllis said as she gave Meredith a hug.

"I'll be a chemist, Phyllis," Meredith thought but did not speak out. She just nodded and smiled to Phyllis.

℅

By Wednesday mid-morning Meredith's hands began to ache. A funeral for a well-known community member was scheduled for 2 p.m. The shop put together three arrangements for the church that would also get transported to the cemetery for a ceremony there. By phone they received orders for three other plants that were to go to the home of the wife of the deceased.

"I have a lot to learn about doing all this transporting, Dena."

Dena just arrived back to the shop after delivering plants and flowers to the deceased's home where a reception was planned after the ceremony. She took a phone call as Meredith took the flower arrangements from the cooler, getting ready to transport to the church.

"We have a problem, Meredith."

Meredith stepped near Dena and looked into her dark brown eyes, "Go ahead."

"Well, the wife of the deceased just called. Now she wants flowers on top of the casket at the church, she doesn't care what color. It's a closed casket now; visitation was last night at the mortuary. She wants us to call her back to let her know we can do this. Then the flowers will go to the graveside on top of the casket."

Meredith searched Dena's eyes, "Babe, we have to satisfy the customer. Of course we'll do it; what we have left in the big cooler is mostly white flowers. Call her back and tell her there will be an arrangement of white flowers on top of the casket. And find out where the casket is, whether it's left the mortuary."

℘

Dena and Meredith laughed and laughed.

"We will not," they both giggled, "tell Phyllis how this went down."

Meredith scrunched down in the back end of the hearse. The casket sat there awaiting more flowers for Meredith to arrange on the top of the casket. They parked on a side street two blocks from the church. The back of the flower shop van pulled up directly behind the hearse. The doors sat wide open on the van and the hearse. Dena and Meredith improvised a beautiful white flower arrangement using white iris, gladioli, and mounds of white carnations. The hearse driver helped them sort flowers by size. Soon they had him laughing.

"Death is a time of celebration, of the accomplishments and joys a person had, so Mr. Smithson, we celebrate your life, well lived. You would approve of the way your casket appears; we just hope your wife approves."

Meredith looked from Dena to the driver as she spoke out. They all laughed together and clapped their hands.

"We have a half hour 'til ceremony," Dena breathed out as she wheeled the van from the side street and headed for the church entrance.

They still had the three flower arrangements to leave at the church for Mr. Smithson's service. The women hustled the arrangements inside and found out where they were to be placed.

"I am so sorry about the wife's last minute plea for casket flowers," the kind reverend said as he nodded to them.

"Reverend," Dena smiled to him and then flashed a smile over to Meredith, "we handled it. I think you'll be pleased."

"Ladies," he patted each of them on the shoulder, "I'm always so happy with the loveliness we see from The Flower Shop, thank you."

They raced out of the church as the first mourners started to get out of their cars and make their way up the church steps.

"Wow, just in time," Meredith breathed out.

"Yeah, that happens to us a lot," Dena chuckled as she nodded to Meredith.

On the way back to the shop Meredith spoke out, "You know what, that was fun. I never did anything like that when I worked at the shop in high school."

"You minded the store, young lady; that was real important. Your mom and me, we did all this messing around; we did have a lot of fun together."

"I'm so glad, 'cause my mom always seemed so serious."

"Meredith, I think your mom came into her own at the shop; she liked the work, the pace, and especially the sense of accomplishment we all felt at the compliments we got for our beautiful work. There's something real peaceful about working with flowers."

"Dena, I think mom and you and Phyllis, well I think of you as artisans, kinda like painters, except you paint with flowers and arrangements."

"I like that, yeah, we are artisans."

℘

After dinner that Thursday night Meredith plunked down on the floor of her bedroom. She just went through her closet looking at her clothes, and adding some beautiful ones. What she always wore never really mattered to her before. But tonight at dinner her dad asked a big favor of her.

"Honey, go through your mom's closet. You two wear the same size, remember how you used to wear some of each other's clothes?"

"I do remember that; mom didn't have a lot of clothes, but they all were very nice. She knew good quality, and Dad, she looked so good in her clothes."

"Your mom is a beautiful woman, Meredith, you have many of her features," Meredith's dad spoke, a sad tone to his voice.

"I have good stuff, genes, from you, Dad, in your defense."

"Thank you," Jack chuckled to his daughter.

"So, what do you want me to do besides go through her stuff?"

"If you find clothes that you like, and that fit you, please take them. That was kinda your mom's intent, to leave some things to you. Please clear her closet and her drawers. I've put a couple of boxes in the bedroom. When you put her things in them, I'll take the boxes and put her name on them, along with the contents, just in case she wants anything. Heck, she may even come back."

Meredith saw her dad nod his head, his eyes looking up and ahead as if he searched for some answer. Then tears came into his eyes as Meredith spoke.

"It's time, to move on, Dad," she patted his upper arm as she walked to her parent's bedroom.

She had in her mind the kind of clothes she might need, not just for the moment, but down the road while she was in college, and later. Meredith spent over an hour going through her mom's lovely things, trying on eight outfits and picking them all. As her dad requested, she boxed her mother's remaining items for her dad to put in storage. Meredith wanted several pretty dresses for the six weddings at which she and Dena were to assist. She now had those dresses, thanks to her mom leaving them at the farm.

℘

The Lund-Micaelson wedding occurred on Saturday of Meredith's first crazy week at the shop. Meredith watched as Dena took the lead on all the wedding details. Meredith approved of the simple flower decorations they created on the church pews and at the front of the church. The bride chose to wear flowers in her hair, so The Flower Shop did not create her a bouquet, just a circle of flowers for her head. The centerpieces at the reception, held in the community room of the wedding church, were similar to the simple flowers at the church. Meredith liked the bride and her sense of simple, but elegant taste in everything about her wedding.

"Dena, someday, if and when I get married, these are the simple, thoughtful arrangements I would want for my wedding."

"Yeah, this bride is older, and has more sense. You will not believe the stuff we're gonna hafta do for a couple of these weddings coming up. Seems like the younger the bride, the more chaos, especially from the bride's mom."

"Maybe the mothers are having the weddings they did not have for themselves."

Dena stood in the shop, her hands on her hips, smiling to Meredith, "Girl, how did you get to be so smart for a kid as young as you are, huh?"

Meredith chuckled to her, "Dad says he stoked me with common sense when I was little, guess it paid off."

૭૭

"We're a great team, Meredith. The church and reception hall are ready, along with the corsages and the boutonnieres. We placed the flowers around the bottom of the cake. You really bust you butt when it gets down to the wire, thanks."

Dena smiled to her, and they hugged.

Dena and Meredith took one last look over their flower handiwork and headed for the room where they changed into their more professional outfits. They wore their gold name badges with The Flower Shop written out above their first names. Never before had Meredith felt more pride in wearing her badge.

"I really can see what I can accomplish," she whispered to herself as she watched the bride and her attendants walk toward them.

Meredith never saw the bride before, and she was super upset, her forehead wrinkled and her eyes tearing.

The bride spoke out in a loud voice, "What am I going to do, what, what?"

Dena approached her, and the bride raised her right arm. She had torn out the underside of the sleeve of her beautiful gown. There was a four inch hole where the seam split. Meredith remembered the kit her mother always carried as they did their weddings. In it were needles, thread in several shades of white and ivory, and scissors.

"I've got this handled, Kristen," Meredith said in a calm voice to the bride as she smiled to the bride.

Within ten minutes Meredith sewed the sleeve, going across the seam three times, to make sure it held.

Kristen required help to repair her makeup from crying. By that time Meredith had finished.

"Thank you, thank you, I know why I had wedding planners; you are miracle workers. I have every confidence that this will come off without another hitch. I love him so much."

She spoke out to Dena and Meredith and then hugged them.

Three hours later the wedding planners emerged from the reception festivities. They ate delicious snacks and tiramisu wedding cake, and even drank a toast of champagne to the bride and groom. They danced to the music of the lively DJ, both with each other and with guys who asked them.

"That was so much fun," Dena smiled to Meredith as they got their gear ready in the van.

"Someday, Dena, there will be a guy I'll love and want to do a wedding with. But that's a long time from now."

Tyler's smiling face flashed in front of Meredith's eyes.

"My special friend, Tyler, at school, I sure do really like that dude. I am in love with him, but it's so far in the future with him. What about you?"

Meredith watched a big smile appear on Dena's face, her deep brown eyes sparkling, "Meredith, some one day for me, down the road, too much going on now in my life."

They hugged after they took their after-wedding gear into the shop and headed out to their cars.

"A day off tomorrow, finally, what a week, right girl?"

Meredith nodded her weary head and drove home.

&

"Colin, I gotta tell you what's on my heart."

Cole sat with his brother in the back yard of the farm home they shared, part of the estate from their parents. They saw corn growing everywhere they looked past the yard.

"I, uh, Meredith, I can't get her out of my thoughts and out of my blood. She excites me like no other woman I've ever known. Jesus all mighty, I hold Ginny Ann in my arms, but it's Meredith I love, now that's the second time I've thought about that. The first time was when I saw Meredith at her house the Sunday she got home from school. I drove away from her so damn upset."

Colin put his hand on his brother's knee and looked into his eyes, "Man oh man, dude, you're marrying Ginny Ann. She'll be moving in with you, as soon as she starts to feel better. You're gonna have a kid before long. I hope you have love for her, for Ginny Ann. Meredith is someone whose mind you could not touch, could not ever have. That's where your excitement comes from. You want what you sure as hell can never have. I'd tell you to grow up, but dude, you already are. You gotta let this fixation go. If this is a prayer, like to God, you're prayin', it's the wrong thing to be prayin'."

His eyes pierced Cole's as he shook his head to his brother.

"I can't stop thinking about Meredith."

Colin watched Cole's eyes fixate on the ground.

"Cole, what are you gonna do?"

Cole threw up his hands and shook his head to Colin, "Marry Ginny Ann on Thursday, sometimes I don't want to live anymore, Colin, sometimes I feel like I want to be with dad. He's in a better place, so's mom."

"Taking your own life is not a good solution to your situation, Cole. Please don't go there. Want me to take you to talk to someone, the minister that's gonna marry you, or someone? Dude, you need help."

"Don't you say nothin' to Ginny Ann," Cole gave his brother an angry glare.

"Gosh Cole, she's been so sick through her first trimester, I'm not gonna say a word. I just hope she feels good enough to walk down the aisle to marry you."

"Colin, she's gotten so gross, gained so much weight, the baby too, I wonder now how I ever could possibly have wanted to screw her, I think I was out of my mind. And now this, a kid, for craps sake."

He raised his head and looked Colin in the eye.

"This whole thing is," Cole paused, and looked up, "God, I'm prayin' to you again, just fix this. Where in the hell was my head during all this time?"

Cole shook his head to his brother.

"Bro, my penis ruled; I will marry her, the right thing to do."

Colin watched his brother's tortured red face, huge tears streaming down onto his shirt.

ℂ

Another week went by for Meredith. She decided it felt pretty wonderful to get a paycheck from the shop. During that time she worked out how she would continue attending K State in the fall. Through a series of calls she and her advisor picked a correspondence class she would enroll in for the fall semester. No one wanted her to have to reapply for school. She checked with her dad to see if she could use his barn office to study in for the class. He agreed that would work. He devoted his fall to harvesting his corn, not spending a lot of time working on the books or making phone calls.

Meredith forgot to pick up the mail from the mailbox on Saturday of that week. Monday morning she remembered because her dad had outgoing mail. She brought in the mail and left it on the counter. She had a letter and a card both addressed to her. One was from Tyler. The card had no return address on the envelope. She took it to her room and put it on her desk for later. She put Tyler's letter in her backpack to read at lunch.

Dena and Meredith worked for several hours that morning on plans for the wedding coming up Saturday.

"This one's gonna be a lollapalooza."

Meredith shook her head and laughed to Dena, "What the heck does that mean?"

"A lot of hard work; we're at a church in Porttown for the wedding and then the reception is held at a country club a few miles away."

By noon they put the final plans together for the Saturday wedding.

"I'm going to run across to the park to eat my lunch, Dena. Then I'll cover for you."

"Good, I've got an errand to do on my lunch break when you get back."

Meredith sat at a park bench. Sunlight streamed down and warmed her from the coolness of the shop air conditioning. She ate several bites of her pb&j and opened Tyler's letter.

Dear Meredith, Wow, I miss you. Unbelievable how much our talks and time together this last semester mean to me. We, well, shared a lot of stuff about each other. Our talks, something. Camp's busy. I think about you a lot. I really want friendship with you. I would like to have your lovely light to guide me as I do my last years at State; then it's so much of an unknown, if it's pilot training, or if it's engineering someplace, cross services with the Army Corps of Engineers, or the Seabees. There are so many different ways I could go.

I know in the fall your light won't be here with me at school; but I still can fly to see you at your farm, and then in the spring, you'll be back! I'll call you once camp's done. I love you. Tyler

Meredith sprinted back to the shop and relieved Dena. The shop remained busy until about 4:30. There was a lull, and Dena took a phone call.

Meredith watched as Dena's eyes bulged when she returned to the back with an order that had lots of writing on it.

"Meredith, sit down. We have to talk."

Meredith continued to stand in front of Dena. She saw tears in Dena's eyes.

"That was a mortuary in town. We'll be handling the flowers for a graveside service coming up on Thursday morning."

"OK, this will be my first graveside," Meredith smiled, thinking of a funeral outside, in the sunshine, in a beautiful setting, with the hills in the background and the trees all around.

Dena walked up to Meredith and put her arms around her.

She spoke in a soft tone, "Meredith, you know the deceased, it's Cole Sanderson."

Meredith let go of Dena. She sat down on the desk chair in the back.

"Is there anyone out front?"

"No."

"Do you have any details, Dena?"

"Only that it's a possible suicide."

Meredith teared up, "Oh my gosh, Dena, he just got married last Thursday morning."

Dena shook her head, "I'm not even gonna try to go there. Didn't you date him?"

Meredith nodded to Dena, "I did sort of; he was so much older, cripes, he kept asking me to marry him, kept saying he loved me."

She stopped, trying to gather her thoughts. She raised her hands up, "He did not understand what the word no meant."

"I'm trying to remember," Meredith watched Dena's forehead wrinkle as she concentrated, "didn't he come back from university to take over the farm operation when his folks got sick?"

Meredith nodded her head, "He did; his mom had early Alzheimer's and his dad had cancer, both gone way early. He runs the operation with his brother, Colin. Cole ran the farm alone while Colin finished up at Iowa State. Cole sacrificed finishing his college education so his younger brother could finish his degree."

"Meredith, are you OK, wanna talk about this?"

Meredith nodded, anger sparked in her eyes as Dena looked at her. Dena heard an angry tone in her voice.

"I felt and still feel that suicide is the ultimate act of selfishness. It was not his time."

Meredith shook her head, her voice strained, "Don't say a word, but the one time I saw Cole when I got home, well he stopped by on Sunday, a day after I got home. He told me that the girl he was marrying was pregnant with his child."

Dena raised up her arm as Meredith got up.

"Meredith, I AM going to say a word about Cole. You said it was not Cole's time. We don't know that. We don't know what God's plan was for Cole. We can't judge, no, it's not our place."

Meredith watched Dena's dark eyes grow bigger and bigger as she made her statement.

"Dena, you're right of course, judge not, lest ye be judged," Meredith came up to Dena as she began to calm down.

They hugged again. Work commenced as they planned for the funeral flowers and the Saturday wedding. They closed the shop right at 5 p.m.

On the drive from town to her farm Meredith reviewed her relationship with Cole. He always said he had a good time with her. It didn't seem to matter what they did together. He always told her he just wanted to be near her. That memory brought tears to her eyes.

She fixed spaghetti and meatballs, garlic bread and salad for all of them for supper. Conner ran late, so Meredith fixed big plates for Uncle Milt and him to heat up when they got home.

"Dad, it's terrible about Cole," she said as they sat eating.

"Just awful, he's leavin' a hell of a mess behind, a new wife and a kid coming. I always liked Colin; now he'll take over the whole farm operation."

"Dad, Colin can handle it; he's smart, has common sense, Cole just never got it through his thick skull about me. I never loved the guy; he was obsessed, that's the word, obsessed over me. That's crazy, don't you think?"

"Meredith, I've known a couple guys like that, one was so crazy he killed his girl, she wasn't even his wife yet. He thought she was cheatin' on him. Some men," her dad shook his head, "just crazy. You look beat; I'll clean up."

"Thanks, Dad," she gave him a tired-eye, weary smile.

Meredith went to her room, grabbed the card she hadn't opened and lay down on her bed. First she reread Tyler's letter.

"Tyler, you are so special to me. But what do I know, I'm 16 years old, and love's gonna change as I get older," she spoke out.

She opened the other card and looked at the front of the card, a painting of a beautiful red rose bud, just beginning to open up.

I love you, Meredith. By the time you read this I will be in another place. I'll be waiting for you, for you to join me when God's ready to bring you home. I can't get you out of my mind; my thoughts circle always back to you. There is a place inside of me that won't let you go. I believe there's a place inside of you that still holds me dear. I truly believe that. I will never forget you, my beautiful wonderful Meredith. Cole

"Oh my dear God. God help me get through this. Should I have seen signs?" she kept asking herself as she jounced off her bed.

"Daddy, daddy where are you?"

"Here Meredith, in the living room on the couch."

"Honey, what's wrong?"

Meredith burst into tears and handed him the red rose card. He read through it once and then again and again a third time.

Meredith nodded to him, "It came in the mail Saturday, but I did not get the mail until today, Monday morning before work. You had outgoing mail. So I brought the mail in and put it on the counter, like always. I had a card and a letter, the letter from Tyler. I left the card on my desk, and I just now read it."

"He made a last very deliberate effort to let you know how he felt," her dad's eyes pierced hers.

"Yes, he did, and I feel terrible."

Jack saw her daughter's drawn colorless face.

"Meredith, sweet pea," she heard a hint of sympathy in her dad's voice.

"I know, Dad, I can read your mind. This is evidence for the suicide investigation regarding Cole's death. This doesn't belong to me anymore."

"We know what we must do."

"Right Dad, I will take this card to the sheriff's office tomorrow morning and make a statement. I need to do this by myself."

Meredith started to cry; her tears came hard and fast.

"Oh my gosh, Dad, if he did not leave a suicide note, this may be all the sheriff will have to go by. I hope they don't have to tell Cole's wife about this letter. She's devastated enough and so sick."

"Meredith, you're thinking is straight and honest. All you can do is turn in your evidence. The rest of it is out of your hands."

"In God's hands?"

Meredith got up, and her Dad came to her. They hugged.

"Yes, honey, in God's hands."

"I'll pray for his family; I'll attend the graveside."

ΕΟ

Meredith called into the shop the next morning and explained that she needed to take part of the morning off, a personal matter. She wheeled her car into the parking lot of the Sheriff's department. Within fifteen minutes she gave her card to the deputy. He took notes as he questioned her about her relationship with Cole.

"I am sorry; I guess I'm more upset than I realized," she apologized to the deputy because she had to stop twice during her answers. She cried hard.

"Sir, I hope you will not have to share this information with Cole's new wife."

"I can't answer that, Meredith, but I would hope that would be the case. Our understanding is that his wife is struggling with the pregnancy."

"Keeping Cole's and Ginny's families in my thoughts and prayers," Meredith nodded to him.

The deputy got up from his chair as Meredith stood up. He shook her hand and thanked her for coming in with the card.

ΕΟ

Meredith and Dena delivered the two flower arrangements to the cemetery an hour and a half before Cole's funeral. Meredith smelled the fresh mowed grass. The earth displaced by the hole for Cole's casket even gave off an odor of new life. Meredith looked around at the trees whispering in the wind.

"What a grand place to rest, this is where Grams and Gramps are, too," she spoke out to the wind.

They returned to the shop; Meredith changed into a pretty summer dress of her mother's. She wore a white summery hat that she saw her mom wear once to an outdoors daytime party. Back at the grave site she took her place standing behind Cole's family. Ginny Ann's mother held one side of Ginny Ann and her dad held her other side as they walked to Cole's casket. Ginny Ann touched the casket and then got escorted away, too sick to stay for the ceremony. Colin saw Meredith standing behind the family. He gave her a smile and a small wave. At the end of the brief ceremony, Reverend invited the group to an immediate reception in a meeting room of the church. Colin found her after the ceremony.

"Meredith, please come to the reception. He always loved you; Ginny Ann is too sick to attend. Will you, for me, stand in, he wanted you to be his wife."

Meredith saw big tears standing in Colin's eyes.

"Of course, Colin, I'll be there," Meredith nodded, with a sympathetic tone that he could hear.

Colin touched her shoulder; Meredith saw thanks in his teary eyes. On her way to her car she stopped by her grandparents' graves. She touched the one headstone, with both their names. Their caskets lay in the ground next to each other.

"Gramps and Grams, we're struggling down here, watch over us, take care of us, like God is, please," she whispered as tears washed down her face.

℘

A quiet reception took place at a meeting room in the church facility. A small group gathered to remember Cole. Church volunteers served cake and punch. Colin, an aunt on his mother's side, and several cousins spoke to the guests as Cole's family circulated through the room. Ginny's parents arrived. They let the group know they just came from the hospital where a decision was made to admit Ginny. The medical folks needed to bring her dehydration, high blood pressure, and pregnancy-driven diabetes under control. Ginny's family could no longer care for her at home.

Colin drew Meredith aside to a quiet corner of the room.

"Once things settle down and in conjunction with our family's lawyer, I want to visit with you, Meredith. There are a couple of things my conscience tells me I need to let you know about Cole. I also need your dad's advice so I'll make some time when he has time."

Meredith nodded and caught Colin's eyes with her own.

"And I as well, have something to share with you about Cole; both of us need time to absorb all this, so so sorry Colin, know that you all are in my thoughts and prayers. Dad sends his regards also."

"Thank you, Meredith, I'll call. I appreciate you being here."

Colin stepped forward and took Meredith in his arms. They remained in a silent hug.

She let him go, "Take care, hear?"

3

A fog enveloped Meredith's mind for a time. She felt a mist wash over her day after day. The mist faded away, and then it came back, hours later.

"My thinking's muddled," she told Dena after their workday was half over on Monday. "Honest, I don't remember working the wedding on Saturday. Did it go well, what da ya think?"

"Meredith, it was a crazy day; went AOK. This deal was a young bride with a mother who wanted an over-the-top event that the mother didn't have herself. You let me lead, and you did everything I asked you to, no questions. You are a super-duper teammate, girl," Dena gave her a hug. "I sense kinda what you are going through."

"Cole's death affects me more than I could ever imagine. Somehow I feel responsible."

"Grief is strange and works on everyone in a different way. I'll just say this once, Meredith. Maybe talk to your minister or a counselor, 'cause two people are absent from your life now."

Meredith gave her a blank look. She shook her head.

"Your mom, Meredith, and Cole. Those people cared for you."

Meredith nodded to her.

"And I cared for them, loved them, I guess now I begin to realize how much. And you're right about talking to someone, Dad and Conner talk to a counselor, I should go."

℘

Colin called Meredith later that week. He also made an appointment with Jack Raymer. He scheduled the meeting before he sat down with the family lawyer about the future of the Sandstrom family trust and the corn farm. Meredith invited him for dinner. That way Colin could relax, have a meal, and spend as much time as he needed to with Meredith's dad.

Meredith heard lots of laughter ring through the dining room at the Raymer home the evening Colin came to dinner. Uncle Milt, Conner, Jack, Meredith and Colin exchanged stories about their earlier days on their respective farms. Meredith fixed coffee to go with their cherry pie.

"I want you guys fortified for your talk," Meredith smiled as she looked from one man to the next.

Conner helped her clean up in the kitchen. They joined the others in the living room where a lively discussion took place.

Colin's eyes moved from one Raymer man to the next. He had his notes about what he wanted to ask. He also brought the business plan Cole drew up some months before, while Colin completed his last semester at State.

"Sir, I would like Milt and Conner to stay with us for a bit, Meredith, you too, if you like. I think all of you will have valuable insights on how I go on from here with the corn operation.

"Colin," Jack spoke up, "we'll try, sum up the business plan for us, OK?"

"I'll try," Colin looked around and swallowed hard, "this reminds me of my ag business project. I don't have a PowerPoint for you, and basically Cole just explained it to me a few months ago."

Meredith watched him as he tried to smile.

Jack Raymer laughed, and they all joined in.

"Ah, son, we don't need no PowerPoint; you'll explain just fine. We just need to listen to you; I'll take a few notes as you go. Plus I'd like to come over to your farm to visit with you and see the progress of your corn."

"I'd like that Jack, you too Milt and Conner. Thanks for taking the time to do that with me," Colin nodded and smiled to them.

Meredith excused herself to prepare for work the next day. She checked her calendar and realized that she did not have a wedding on Saturday. That meant the shop closed at 2 p.m. She had almost a day and a half free. Meredith rejoined the men in the living room and refilled their cups, this time with decaf coffee. She noticed how Conner paid close attention to what Colin said, Conner's eyes keen on Colin's face.

"God, you gave me a very special brother," she prayed. "I'm amazed at what he continues to accomplish," she nodded her head.

"Thanks, all of you, for your insights and recommendations about a couple of changes to the plan," Colin's eyes moved from face to face to face. "I am grateful for the good people around me," he nodded and tried to smile.

80

Meredith and Colin moved to the back yard and sat at the patio chairs with their sodas. The lights from the living room shone out the French doors, giving them ample light.

"You start, Meredith, you told me at the reception that you needed to talk to me."

"Cole sent me a card, a beautiful card with a red rose on the front. It seemed he wrote it as he planned his death. I got the card on a Saturday; he died that day?"

"Right, that's what the medical examiner determined."

"Cole wrote that he loved me, that by the time I got the card he would be in another place. He wrote that he would be waiting for me to join him, when it was my time."

Meredith stopped talking. She put her hands over her face and cried. After a little she settled down and took her hands away and placed them on the table. She mopped up her face and nose with a tissue. Colin took her hand and held it softly in his own as he continued to look at her.

"He wrote that there was a place inside of him that wouldn't let me go and he thought that there was a place inside of me that held him dear. He said he truly believed that. He said he'd never forget me."

Colin looked into her eyes, awash with tears again.

Meredith watched him nod his head to her.

"That's pretty much the way he explained his love for you to me."

"Colin, he married someone else."

Colin raised his hand, "This is all I can tell you, he married, well, there's a baby coming."

Meredith watched his face as he began to tear up.

"Oh Colin, I will continue to pray for you. I showed dad Cole's card. He said I was doing the correct thing to take it to the Sheriff's office. One of the deputies interviewed me the next morning when I turned the card over as evidence. This is a tough question, which you don't have to answer."

"Meredith, I know what you're going to ask."

Colin took a deep breath and released it slowly. Meredith thought she could even hear his pain release as he breathed out.

"No, there was no suicide note. It does my heart good to know he communicated with someone. I have to tell you, I asked if I could help him, refer him to a counselor, or something. He sought no help, just married Ginny."

Colin lowered his head and started to shake it.

"It's unbelievable what's happening to Ginny, she's gaining so much weight; the docs say the baby's growing way too fast. I'm praying she makes it; baby too, she's very ill. The wedding presents still sit in a spare bedroom at the farm. They haven't been opened. It was everybody's hope that Ginny would start to feel better. But even on their wedding night, Cole and Ginny agreed that she was not ready to move into our home. He took her back to her home and came back here. There was no honeymoon."

"Oh, Colin, you've been through so much."

"Yeah, but God, he's got somethin' goin' on for me. I sure as hell don't know what his plan is," he shook his head, "but I must move forward. The corn is growing. With what your dad and uncle talked to me about, there are a couple of changes that I need to make. I tell you what I fear; I fear failure, like if something happens to the corn crop, or I screw something up in what I think Cole might want me to do."

Colin paused and took a deep breath. Meredith watched his eyes look out, over the land. He shook his head.

"I've had no luck with women; honest to pete, when I tell them I run a corn operation, they just turn away. Seems like nobody wants to be a farmer's wife any more. I just haven't seen many good relationships between men and women, my parents so sick, your mom wanting out of the farm life, poor Ginny, willing to take on a farm, but her getting sick, too."

"If there are things I could help with, Colin, I would like too," she directed her eyes to his.

Colin nodded to her, his eyebrows raised, "Yeah, Meredith, your dad said the same thing to me. Yes, I will ask for help. Cole handled it all as he watched our parents die so young, made me stay in school, always told me, 'Bro, learn everything you can, utilize all the ag training they're gonna give you, you'll need it, to manage everything here.'"

"Sage advice."

"Yeah, but didn't think I'd need to be using that training, like right away."

"I've work tomorrow, so I'll say goodbye, but let me tell you that I also fear failure."

She stopped what she was saying and looked him full in the face. "Everythins' been handed to me, all my life. Now, well I see how life really works, the drudgery of working a job, trying to hold a family together. I know it's not my job, really to do all that, but I feel I must, until I go back to school. I'm afraid I won't be able to teach these men in my life how to cope without me. So I'm like a scared little kid, so scared I may fail."

Meredith shook her head to him as she got up and walked with him into the house. He handed her his glass and she put both of them in the dishwasher. Colin looked around at the neat, homey arrangement of the Raymer home.

He gazed at Meredith as they stood together by the front door.

"I feel it here, Meredith, your home, a place with a lot of love filling these rooms, a lot of love, you have so much to do with that," he nodded and then came to Meredith for a hug.

"G'night, now Meredith," he whispered in her ear. He smelled her hair and her light perfume. It surprised him how he felt his groin tighten.

"Be safe driving home and take care," she spoke to him as they stepped away from their hug.

SO

That night Meredith tried to review some of her chemistry, going over her lecture notes. Her thoughts kept straying, and she was not tired. She decided to go for a walk with Jeepers. She looked up into the star-filled sky as she talked in a quiet tone to the dog.

"What 'cha think Jeepers, will I see Tyler before long?"

She stopped walking and knelt down on one knee as Jeepers looked up at her.

"So, what's your answer?"

Jeepers raised up his right paw.

"I guess that means soon, huh?"

Jeepers gave her a sloppy kiss on her cheek.

"Thanks, Jeepers."

They continued their walk down the open area between the corn fields. The moon shone bright, lighting the sky. Meredith watched a few high white clouds skittering by. She breathed in, a deep breath, held it, and in slow fashion exhaled out.

"You'll be getting tired, Jeepers, let's head home."

The lights of her home shone as they approached it. Meredith felt a calm and a lifting of her spirits.

"Thanks, Jeepers for walking with me; it helped me realize that I am happy right now, here at my own home. My wanting to get away and have whole new experiences, that feeling is not so dramatic now, that need not so intense."

She walked him to Uncle Milt's and knocked on the door to his place.

"Thanks, Meredith for taking Jeepers for a walk."

She smiled to her uncle, "We had a good time; he's sure a good listener."

Uncle Milt laughed and she added her chuckle.

ℰ✺

Meredith checked her calendar. Tyler finished summer camp. She kept thinking about him, and his wish to visit her. She knew he would call when he could. Before bed that night she took a good look at her home. The family had very few guests stay overnight. Meredith remembered sleepovers she had with her girlfriends from school, centuries ago. She looked around the guest bedroom. The bedspread needed washing, and the carpet needed vacuuming. Meredith discovered only a mattress pad under the bedspread. She searched through the family's meager linen closet. She started a list and took it to her dad who worked on his books out in his barn office.

"I know Tyler is planning to visit us. Dad, I need to buy sheets for the guest bedroom. I'll clean the room up real good for his visit."

"Mom probably took the sheets for California," he shook his head. Meredith noticed his sad tired eyes.

"Here, this should cover it; check our pillowcases. Buy new ones if you need too."

He handed her money, and Meredith thanked him.

"I'll pick these up after my half day Saturday at the shop. G'night dad, sleep well."

They hugged.

"Yeah, I'm sleeping better; letting yesterday go, trying hard each day." He smiled a weary smile to her, "Lookin' forward to a great corn crop; conditions just super."

"Glad to hear it, Dad," her voice cheered him as did her shining eyes.

℘

Meredith loved the quiet weekend. Saturday afternoon she picked up the sheets at a local store and took them, the mattress pad and the bedspread to a laundry. She sat in the back listening to the tumble of the laundry drying as she read an interesting magazine about Hollywood stars. She saw blurbs about a couple of movies that just came to the screen. When she got home, she opened the drapes in the guest bedroom, gave them a quick vacuum and dusted the small chest, then did the carpet. She straightened up the closet and put hangers there for a guest.

"Wow, looks nice, girl, you do good work," she said out loud as she patted herself on the back. The room smelled of fresh linen after she made the bed and put on the bedspread.

"I'm ready for you, Tyler, to visit."

She nodded her head as she walked down the hall and back to the kitchen. Her mind whirled as she thought ahead to a family dinner for Tyler and a picnic for just the two of them. She remembered a place she visited with her Girl Scout troop a few years back.

෨

Meredith ran to the small plane as she watched him wave to her. Tyler stood nearby with a bag.

"Wow, I missed her more than I could imagine," he spoke out as he saw the red-shirted, blue-jeaned figure charge toward him. Her hair flew out behind her, and she smiled her brilliant smile to him. They stayed in their hug for a long time. They gave each other a soft kiss, then a longer one, exploratory, moving their lips across each other's.

Meredith felt a sexual burning in her groin as she felt Tyler's body holding tight against hers.

"Missed you," Tyler pulled back and looked into Meredith's eyes.

"Missed you more," Meredith smiled to him as they walked together to her car.

They talked and talked as Meredith drove Tyler to the farm from the small county airport. She showed him to his room and let him get settled in. Meredith started dinner. She decided on a large pork roast which cooked in the oven.

"Can I help?" Tyler asked as he walked into the kitchen.

"Yeah, here's a potato peeler, and here are the potatoes. Go to it."

They chatted as they worked together at the kitchen sink.

"This place is like your chemistry lab, everything so nice and neat?"

She smiled to Tyler, and paused in reflection, "Yeah, it really is, this is my food lab, place I build nice meals, good eatin'."

Tyler stopped her in the middle of her making the salad. He put his hand under her chin and moved her face to his. He gave her a slow, deep kiss, tongues touching. Meredith felt the ache from the kiss build, from her toes to the top of her head.

"Wow, my pilot, oh wow," her eyes widened at the power of his kiss.

"Yup, wow, I feel it too," his eyes blazed into hers.

ℰ

She walked with him down a field of corn, just outside the back lawn of the Raymer property. She tried to give him a quick summary of the progress of the corn.

"This is, for sure, your world, Meredith, you speak like you really enjoy the corn growing," Tyler stopped her and looked into her eyes.

"I, I guess, I do, it's such a part of me, in my blood, the agriculture part of me, it's all I've ever known, 'til I went to State," she nodded to him, a smile forming on her face.

Tyler touched her cheek with his hand, "You don't dislike it as much as you used to talk about, right?"

"You're right, it's my life now, helping my family, and it's what I have to do until January of next year. I might as well make the best of it. Hey, the meat should be cooked, so we'll all eat in a few."

They walked back inside her home as the doorbell rang. Meredith let go of Tyler's hand as she strode across the living room to answer the door.

"Oh my God, Meredith, may I come in, somethin' terrible's happened."

Meredith held Colin's shoulder and ushered him into the room. She saw tears blinding his eyes. He stumbled into the coffee table in front of the couch.

"Oh, sorry, I got to sit down. Oh Meredith, Ginny Ann died, the baby died, oh my God. What am I, what am I, how to?"

He burst into tears again. Meredith sat next to him and took him in her arms, holding him tight. Tyler stood a few steps back, not understanding, but watching Meredith, seeing the compassion she showed for the man. Just then Jack and Conner Raymer came in through the door from the garage.

Tyler turned to the men and walked up to introduce himself to Jack and Conner.

"Something's happened to the man on the couch," Tyler said in a solemn voice.

Tyler, Jack and Conner found seats in the living room.

As Colin calmed down, Meredith asked Conner to take the meat out of the oven and put tin foil over it to stay warm.

Colin let go of Meredith and accepted tissues.

"Want to tell us, Colin?"

Colin responded to Jack's question. He explained to them that he got a phone call an hour earlier from Ginny Ann's parents. They were still at the hospital. Ginny died from preeclampsia, and the baby was stillborn.

"I'm the only Sanderson now," Colin shook his weary head as he looked around at the group listening to him. "I know you folks heard my farm plan. Now I need to do what I can for Ginny Ann's family. Thank you for being here 'cause I need to be with folks just now."

"We're about to sit down to dinner. Please stay, Colin. You shouldn't be alone, young man."

"Thanks, sir," he tried to smile to Jack.

Tyler carried the dinner conversation that night. His dream to become a pilot looked like it was going to work out. Colin and Conner listened with eagerness to his tales of flying airplanes. After the meal Colin appeared calmer, more stable, in that his explanations of what would happen with Ginny Ann and her family made good sense. And what he had to do back at the farm appeared to be normal farm duties. Jack asked Colin to take Conner home with him to spend the night. No one wanted Colin to be alone at his farm that night.

It was late when Colin and Conner left the Raymer farm. Tyler and Meredith talked just a little about their plans for

Sunday. At church Meredith planned to accompany the choir on her French horn. So Tyler wanted to be with her to hear her play. After that they planned to take a picnic lunch to a small lake near the County Airport. Tyler needed to fly to Lawrence where he would start back at his old job as a mechanic at the small airport near town. His report date was the next day.

"I'll say good night and sweet dreams now, Meredith. That Colin is one super strong dude, he has really been through it, losing parents, brother, now this loss. I can't even imagine death yet. It hasn't happened to any of my family."

Meredith nodded to him. They kissed and went off to their bedrooms. Tyler tossed and turned in his bed. What he observed earlier that evening shook him to his core.

He saw the agony in Colin's face and heard the raw emotion as he spoke. But throughout the dinner, as he talked of his flying adventures, Tyler noted something else. Meredith seemed unaware of it, but Tyler saw, again and again, the loving looks Colin gave Meredith. Tyler figured that they knew each other for many years before as little farm kids and then as school kids. It sounded like Colin's farm operation was not far away from the Raymer farm operation.

"I have competition; someone else loves her too. It'll be so many years from now before Meredith and I can be together. I think, maybe, we will not end up together."

That thought whirled through his brain until sleep came to him.

ℰↃ

"Wow, Meredith, your horn playing, it was so good. I'd never heard you play, honest, did you ever even tell me you had a music background?"

Meredith turned her eyes from the road to him as she smiled, "Uh, probably not. There was so much other stuff to talk about, you and me."

"Your congregation sure seems happy to have you back, the compliments. They all sure made me feel welcome."

Back at the farm they scooted around, getting their picnic ready. Tyler packed his gear. They would go from their picnic to his plane. As Meredith drove to the lake for the picnic, she explained the role of wedding planner that she now played as an employee of The Flower Shop.

They laughed over the goofs and gaffs and the beautiful young people in love. That's what happened at the weddings Meredith worked on so far that summer. Both of them agreed that marriage included so many more responsibilities than they ever imagined. As they ate the fried chicken breasts, watermelon and chocolate chip cookies, Tyler talked about summer camp and his responsibilities.

"You're ready to lead, Tyler. And to fly, when will you learn about the pilot slot?"

"Not until I'm a fifth yearer, remember CE takes five years, one more year to go after this one. I'll really have more time to fine tune my flying, get more training on my own. I can do that 'cause of the scholarship money, the extra, that I got from my scholarship, remember, you were there when they awarded it to me."

"Right, I remember, Tyler."

Meredith smiled to him, thinking back on that special night, the Awards Banquet. They sat, listening to the waves lap onto the nearby shore. It was quiet for a time as their thoughts whirled.

Meredith watched Tyler raise his hand and look up into the sky. He pointed to a jet up high. He gave Meredith a smile and spoke, his voice reverberating upward.

"I've topped the windswept heights with easy grace
Where never lark, or even eagle flew,
And, while with silent, lifting mind I've trod
The high untrespassed sanctity of space,
Put out my hand, and touched the face of God."

Tyler looked at Meredith with his serious deep brown, almost black eyes, "John Gillespie Magee, Jr., *High Flight.*"

Meredith nodded her head, "What a poem, Tyler."

He took her hands and held them in his own. They were silent, letting the settling wind pass their warm faces.

"Please date other people, Meredith, I need to, now and in the future. It's a boundary I want to have with you. We cannot be a couple; we have too many years to go, at least three before you'll have your degree. It's important for me, that you date, be happy, explore other people, have fun. Is that OK?"

"Yes, it's a have to, Tyler, but," Meredith looked him in the eye, her eyebrows raised, "when I get back spring semester I hope that I can see you, and see others, but date you too. I LOVE YOU, TYLER," she paused with each word as she emphasized each of the four.

They held in a hug.

"And I love you, Meredith."

80

Meredith watched him taxi down the runway. Once his plane rose to enough altitude, Tyler did a wiggle waggle with his wings. He told her he would, his special goodbye to her.

Tyler thought about how grownup Meredith seemed as he visited at the farm. She did so much more than he ever imagined. She handled her cooking responsibilities with ease. Her home appeared clean and welcoming. Her brother, father and uncle adored her, that was obvious from their eye contact, hugs and mentions of appreciation for her. He saw a lot of caring among all of them while he was in the Raymer home. His biggest surprise remained Colin. Meredith handled him with great maturity. Tyler nodded his head as he looked at the clear skies ahead.

"Colin cares about Meredith, for sure. I felt pretty inadequate as Meredith showed me her world. She just does so much, keeping up a home and a family and her job with the florist, and her musical talent," Tyler spoke out as he headed west for his home. "I need to ask mom if there's stuff I could help her with around my home. My sister helps, but my dad, he's only home on Sundays."

℘

Meredith clapped as she watched Tyler's special goodbye as he sped through the skies.

"I am growing up," she spoke out as she drove back to the farm. "I'm not devastated about Tyler leaving today; sad, but there must be more people in my life besides him. He'll visit again; it may be a long time from now, but he'll visit again, I know it, and it's not forever 'til next January. I gotta invite more love into my life, ah, give up any struggle, with Tyler; it can't just be him in my future. It's like my struggle to get out of my old life; see, my old life is right back with me, and it's OK, I can do this, be happy, help out."

Her mind zoomed in on Colin. His world got turned upside down. She reminded herself she made a promise to help him, if and when he reached out and asked for her help. Colin was rock solid. She always admired him, a serious student in school, an honor graduate in his ag program at State. He held a couple of records in track at Porttown High, in the high hurdles, a good athlete. Meredith wondered about his dating situation. She hoped there was someone he cared about, that he met at State.

She teared up when a thought came to her, "What if there is no one special? Everyone needs someone special in their lives."

She shook her head at that thought. Conner reminded her later that evening that the Fourth of July approached. She had plans with her dad, Conner, and Uncle Milt.

ꙮ

At the last minute Meredith got a call from her high school band director. Mr. Parker also managed the small symphony orchestra he organized in Porttown some years ago. He asked Meredith to fill in for the second chair French horn who got sick a day before the concert. Meredith expressed her concern about sight reading unfamiliar music. He assured her that she could handle the material. So after the late afternoon Fourth of July picnic sponsored by several civic organizations, she played with the Porttown Symphony Orchestra. Her group and three other musical groups after them shared patriotic, rock, and blue grass music for the people of Porttown. Meredith and her family sang *The Star Spangled Banner* before the fireworks display began at Porttown's City Park.

"It was a lot of fun," the family agreed as they returned home, sunburned and happy, after the fireworks concluded.

"Meredith, we heard you and the other French horn in one of the pieces, you sounded great," she saw a wide smile form on her dad's face before she headed off to bed.

ꙮ

The next day, Saturday, Meredith and Dena worked a wedding, their third that summer.

"For sure, Dena," Meredith said to her as they finished up delivering the wedding flowers to the church, "I'm just beginning to figure out what love is all about, and seeing the casts of characters for the weddings we've helped with has certainly opened up my eyes."

"Yeah, we sure've seen last minute hysterics and deep moments of humor in the couples so far. All I gotta say is they must really, REALLY," Dena emphasized the word the second time, "care about each other. I swear I missed seeing love light shining in a couple of sets of eyes, in the weddings so far."

Meredith nodded, thinking back, remembering the couples who married. She shook her head as she thought of all the kinds of emotions that must have hit the couples throughout that special day. Meredith decided that a wedding day was a difficult day for everyone involved in the proceedings. If it was a happy day for the couple, that was the best kind of situation. This wedding picked up on the patriotic theme of the Fourth, so the flowers and the wedding setting and reception saw a big splash of red, white, and blue. Even the tablecloths at the reception were spread out in red, white, and blue. This reception had an element that Meredith had not seen before, an open bar. The dancing got very lively as the amount of booze consumed rose higher and higher. With a little alcohol in their systems, the bride and groom loosened up a bit and participated when almost everyone in the place danced to the line dance. Meredith never had the opportunity to learn line dancing. Dena helped her with a couple of places where she got her feet mixed up.

"That was fun," Meredith concluded, as they left the reception while the caterers did the final cleanup.

"Yes, it was, I was a little worried when the booze started flowing, but I think everyone minded their manners. I did remind one fine-looking tipsy single guy about his conduct at this happy affair. He asked me for my name and took my card, wrote my number on the back for him."

"Hey, I am told, dearie," Meredith smiled to Dena, "that singles do show up for these events, and some dates come out of the deal. Good for you, girl!"

"Meredith, I just wish you were a little older, you're just too young for most of these guys."

Meredith gave Dena a hug, "Yeah, I know, but someday, I'll be just right. And hey, thanks for a super day. This wedding far surpassed what we've done before, and I just don't remember the one after Cole died."

ℬ

Colin sat two rows back of Meredith at church the Sunday after the July Fourth celebration. He talked to God about his situation. Tomorrow he had another funeral to attend, in the afternoon, for both Ginny Ann and her baby.

"Ask for help," is what Colin kept hearing in his head. He tried to tune back in to the events of the church service right before him. It seemed impossible. He kept saying a prayer until the service finished. On the way out he caught up with Meredith.

"God keeps telling me to ask for help. So I'm asking, Meredith. Can you help me sort out what needs to happen at my home, and with me?"

"Of course, Colin," she touched his upper arm and looked him in the eye, "I told you I would; our whole family will help you. That's what friends are for. And our family and yours, well the friendship goes back to our grandparents."

Colin walked Meredith to her car.

"Make a list, Colin, use a calendar," she looked up into his eyes, his 6'2" frame overshadowing her, and Meredith stood tall herself.

She nodded to him, "All the things that need to happen, include your lawyer and his dealings. Between Dad, Uncle Milt, Conner, and me, we should be able to sort out the important items."

Colin reached out to touch her, then stopped.

"And people keep telling me, don't do anything super huge for six months." His blue eyes searched hers, "To me that sounds like such a long time, don't you think?"

Meredith nodded, "Colin, it's just that, uh, sometimes people, in grief, make decisions that they later regret."

"Makes sense, I'll let you go. I'll sit down, go through the homestead, and our surrounding buildings and write everything out. The plan was for me to move out and let

Cole and Ginny have the home. I was about to fix up a small place on our property for me. Now that's all changed."

Meredith watched him shake his head. He started to tear up.

"I need your help right away with something, though, Meredith. I must return the wrapped wedding gifts of Cole and Ginny's that came home after the wedding. I want to do that in person, for several. Could you help return some for me, to folks here in Porttown? And I need three gifts sent back in the mail."

"I can, Colin. Bring the gifts by the shop; I can do some on my lunch break. And the post office is not far."

"Where'd you learn to think like you do, on your feet, thinking so clear?"

Meredith nodded to him. He watched a big smile beam across her face.

"My folks, they always had problems to solve. Conner, me, we put our heads together, all of us, and helped figure out solutions, so mom and dad, yeah, they were great."

"I gotta let you go, pretty chaotic at my house. My mom got in the clutches of Alzheimer's real early. Thanks, Meredith, ahead of time for your help; you'll see when you come to the homestead."

"Colin, you'll be in my thoughts and prayers as you attend yet another funeral. Colin, I believe in you, you can do this."

He heard the steadiness of her voice and saw encouragement in her lovely eyes.

Colin nodded, hugging her. He watched Meredith drive away before he got in his pickup and headed for home.

"Oh, Jesus, dude, I'm beginning to see the depth of Meredith, of what Cole saw. She is so hot; I'm starting to fall for her. She's too damn young for me. And there's another guy."

That thought rolled around in his head for most of that afternoon.

He did what Meredith asked, the list.

2

Tyler, I have kinda a tough time expressing myself in writing, wish I could thank you in person for visiting me. You saw my world, the one I'll have 'til I get back to school. I'm in love with you, Tyler. Some dreams came true when I met you. Deep in my heart there're feelings I have for you, more than love, caring, understanding, unbelievable that you love me. But what is a 16-year-old love? I'm just beginning to understand what love is all about.

I totally get it when you talk about dating others. Committing to another, I can't do that. You understand that, I got three years of college left, then four years (or more) with the Air Force as an officer. I figure I need to be 24 before I can really begin to be in a serious relationship. I do not want to give up the military until I decide I want to. My resolve is NOT to give it up just to marry. So THANK YOU for talking about boundaries, about caring for others, for dating others. I'm just starting to know what I need in a relationship in order for a young man to be in my life.

I want to get to know more and more about you, Tyler, what you care about, what your resolve, your initiative is all about, where you want your dreams for your future to take you.

Love, Meredith

ℰℐ

Meredith put Tyler's letter in the outgoing mailbox on her way to work on Monday. As he said he would, Colin brought seven presents to the flower shop. Meredith found a place for them in the back business area. He gave her the addresses and phone numbers for the presents to be delivered. The gifts that he wanted mailed were to go to the packaging store, he decided, instead of the post office. The store would handle the mailing.

"You'll need this cash and these addresses for the mailings, Meredith. Cheech, I already am starting to feel better about what to do with everything. You were," he nodded his head to her, "wow, so right, about making that list. I organized myself on a calendar for the next three weeks. I have a lot I plan to accomplish, thanks to you."

Colin smiled to her. She watched his expressions as he spoke to her about the list. His eyes shone; she saw gratefulness in them.

"He looks so professional in his suit for the funeral. He'll start to heal, to feel better about himself, his future," Meredith thought. "It's a long process, like me with mom."

ℰℐ

Meredith took three different lunch hours to return packages from Cole's wedding. She got lucky and caught three people at home and one package she delivered to the person's work. All four people broke down and cried about the very difficult circumstances surrounding the deaths of Cole and his family. They all wanted to send out their prayers to Colin, in the hope that he could carry on alone with the farm operation.

Meredith called Colin to let him know she completed her deliveries including those to the packaging store. She told him about the prayers for him from the four people with whom she spoke.

"Thanks, Meredith, man, I need every prayer I can get. I got all the other presents delivered. I've seen the lawyer; the family trust is updated. I have an appointment with a financial advisor at our bank. He'll help me plan for my future and the farm's future. I'm Cole's beneficiary on a life insurance policy he's had for some time, and thank the Lord we are both signers on his personal and family checking accounts. My folks really planned ahead for Cole and me. I don't have any student loans, and Cole took care of all the medical expenses on my folks. So it looks like money isn't an issue, at least right now."

Colin paused, "My folks died fast, without incurring the huge medical expenses most folks have to deal with. I didn't really know what was happening on the home front; Cole kept most of their medical situations to himself. I have a lot of survivor's guilt, like I shoulda done more to help him out while the folks were so sick. I was happy at Iowa State; Cole insisted I stay on. He handled everything. Jesus, Meredith, I am friggin' so sad, right now. And I'm just shaken to my core over all the deaths. I just swim in sorrow."

Meredith heard the increasing tremors in his voice. She started to tear up herself.

"Time and the upcoming corn crop will help take care of your grieving, Colin," she tried to soothe him, "I promise. Since I got home I've been too busy to mourn my mom. She still hasn't contacted Conner or me."

"I'm sorry, Meredith," there was a pause as Colin let out a sigh.

"I'm available Sunday afternoon, if you want me to come over to see what help my family and me can be to you."

"Geez, Meredith, that would be great; what about 1 p.m. You'll have time to get home from church and have lunch."

"Right, see you then."

ଓ

"Family meeting after dinner, OK everybody?" Jack Raymer said to his family as they sat down to dinner Saturday night.

Everyone ate in the quiet; soft country music played in the background. After dishes got cleaned up, Uncle Milt, Jack, Conner, and Meredith sat in the living room. Jack sat between Conner and Meredith. Meredith's dad held paperwork in his hands. He moved his eyes from one person to the next and finally to Meredith. Meredith looked back at him and saw despair pinging from his eyes to hers. His eye color changed from blue to a cold gray.

"Your mother wants out; she wants me out of her life. She told me to take care of it, no contest. She wants no money, just out. I filed for divorce yesterday afternoon. I know it's not what you wanted to hear; I thought we might reconcile, but she says her life is goin' good where she is. I want you two to take good care of yourselves; you did not cause my problem, and you sure as heck can't fix it. It's important that you go to counseling, if you don't do it for yourselves, do it for me. You know I'm in counseling," he paused, his voice trembling now, "and it's helping me. We have suffered a terrible loss."

Meredith watched tears running like rivulets from a rain shower down her dad's cheeks.

"Dad, I'm so sorry," Meredith broke down and put her arm around his shoulder.

Conner put his head into his dad's chest and bawled, louder than he cried for a long, long time. Meredith saw big tears roll down Uncle Milt's face.

"Mom still hasn't called us," Conner lifted his head.

"She says she'll take your calls, so call her."

"Dad, dad," Conner continued to cry, "what, what can I say to her."

"Conner, look at me."

Conner started to calm down.

"This is just a suggestion," Jack paused and looked from Conner to Meredith, "tell her you love her, maybe let her know how sad you feel, maybe let her know that you miss her."

"Thanks, Dad, both Conner and I can do that."

"You two, remember," Jack's eyes filled with tears now, "I will always love her; there is a place in my heart where she'll go on with me."

At that, both Conner and Meredith cried. Jack let the papers lay in his lap. He put an arm around each of his children as they burrowed into his chest. Uncle Milt came around behind the couch where they sat. He put his arms around the three of them and rested the side of his face on top of Jack's head. The crying continued from all four of them for a time.

☙

Colin watched for Meredith's car. He stepped out on his front porch and walked to her. Meredith stood by the car as Colin smiled to her.

"I been meanin' to tell you, Meredith, but there is someone else in my life, always has been."

Meredith gazed up at him. She opened her mouth to speak.

Colin interjected, "God."

"Right," Meredith agreed.

"Hey, He's been standin' right beside me, every day, all my life. It sure as heck took a long time for me to figure it out, three deaths, no, my folks, five deaths."

"You're not alone, Colin."

"No, I'm not, man, am I glad you are here, anxious to get some settlings done. The corn's growing, and time's fleeting."

Meredith tried to smile to him, "Dad told me that he and Uncle Milt came over to advise on stuff. I'm glad you're going to auction off farm equipment that you decided you don't need."

"Cole's pickup, tomorrow I'm trading it and my pickup for a better set of wheels."

"Another pickup?"

"Yeah, but with a heck of a lot better gas mileage; the old things we got are gas guzzlers."

Two hours later Colin and Meredith took a break. He fixed iced coffee for both of them. They sat across from each other at a table out on the back patio. Meredith watched the corn waving lazy leaves to them.

"You'll be able to live with the mess we've created until Goodwill brings out their truck to take everything away?"

"Yeah, I can. Meredith, I'll hire a cleaning person to fix up everything once the stuff is gone. Somethin's bothering me, I don't want to save all the photo albums, but my folks had so many."

"That's stuff you've saved back, right?"

Colin nodded to her.

"Suggestion?"

"Of course, Meredith, need all the input I can get from you."

"Be hard on yourself, know that someone, someday will have to trash what you don't get rid of now."

Colin teared up and paused for a while, "Sheesh, I sure don't want a kid of mine having to toss stuff that means nothing to him or her. So what are you saying about the albums?"

"Pick ten memorable pictures from each album, maybe in like a time order. Take the pics to a photo shop; they can scan them into a video for you to keep. Hey, the shop can put music to the video, maybe a song you remember from your folks' time. Someday I'll suggest that to my dad. But we don't have the number of pictures you guys have."

"You're amazing, Meredith, you know what, you're just about the most special person I know."

Meredith opened her mouth in surprise.

Colin took his hand, reached over and touched her cheek with the back of his hand.

"Thank you, Meredith, and thanks for your suggestions about what to do about the house insides. A while back," he paused, "well, you told me you believed in me. I was so shaky back then. You sure as heck believed in me, when I didn't even believe in myself. Now I'm better; I can accomplish some of what I want to do. I can let the rest go 'til I get to it."

℘

Ten days went by. Meredith realized she needed to talk to someone about her mom. Meredith felt so much anger; she'd been abandoned, so had Conner. They attended an evening meeting with Reverend Hartman at the family's church.

Conner handled the meeting much better than Meredith did. He had previous counseling sessions with his dad and another counselor. Meredith told Reverend about her difficulty. She talked about her anger. Every night she spent at least five minutes punching the living heck out of her pillows.

"This will take time, you two, for you both to get used to the fact that your mother is not returning. But you've told me you both talked to her and that she says she loves you."

Both Conner and Meredith nodded their heads.

"Time, God's love, that will hold you. Eventually you'll see the situation as you need to. One day you may decide to visit her, is that a possibility?"

Again, they nodded their heads.

"As hard as this sounds, you two," Reverend paused and looked into Conner's and then Meredith's eyes, "try to forgive your mom. Forgiveness is important because your anger will flare and get the best of you; to forgive is the balm that will soothe your mind."

Meredith and Conner agreed that they would meet with Reverend, once a month, until Thanksgiving. Reverend had a final suggestion for Meredith.

"If there's a pet in your lives, that could be a comfort to you two."

Meredith and Conner looked at each other and smiled to Reverend.

"Jeepers," they said in unison.

"Uuummm, that's the dog we grew up with," Conner added.

"He's been spending time at Uncle Milt's, who lives close to us, in an apartment in the barn. Both Conner and me thought it best for Jeepers not to be alone in our home, Conner at work all day and me away at school."

"So what do you want to do with Jeepers?"

"Conner, what do you think, Jeepers in your bedroom one night, then mine one night, we can alternate?"

"Yeah, cozy, it'll be cozy to have Jeepers with us."

"Yup," Meredith nodded to her brother, "A comfort, 'cause we're missing our mom."

"Try it, you two," let me know if it helps you, OK?

❧

July disappeared into August. As soon as she could, Meredith started her correspondence class. She needed to satisfy a humanities requirement for her major. She chose an Art through the Ages class. She found the course fascinating with the variety of paintings, sculptures and pottery the instructor used as visual aids. She never paid much attention to history or geography. Now she realized that when and where creations were made was important in the world of art. It was like her knowledge of Chemistry's table of elements and dates and who discovered the newer elements added to the table. Her knowledge base began to expand.

"I am so glad to be back in school," she told her dad often. "I'm using my brain all the time at home and at the shop, but I love the challenge of learning new stuff."

Her dad smiled to her from his place at the breakfast table.

"Dad?"

"Yeah, sweet pea?"

"Colin is struggling at counseling; he thinks it's not helping him. He's pretty angry."

"That's exactly why he needs to go," Jack nodded his head to his daughter.

"He's asked me to come along with him; he says I suffered a loss, too, which I have, mom."

"Whatcha think?"

"I guess it couldn't hurt to go along with him. He's not liking being alone to make all the decisions. It frustrates him, he says. I'm his friend, I should go, friends help friends, right?"

Meredith watched her dad smile, "That's right; just a caution, you gotta take good care of yourself."

Jack got up and patted his daughter's shoulder

ℰℴ

Meredith attended two counseling sessions with Colin. They met at their church with their minister. Colin talked about his sense of loss.

"I still feel a lot of anger, left holding this whole mess."

Meredith looked first to Reverend and then to Colin.

"Maybe it might help you, when I think of my mom now, gone from my life, I don't get angry. I remember what she told me and my brother over the years. Parts of life are hard. She kept telling us to keep trying, keep trying, do our best at what we needed to accomplish. Maybe you can think of your loved ones that way. I know your folks encouraged you; you graduated from college. You do keep trying, now as you put your life in order, waiting for the harvest."

Meredith put her hand over her mouth and looked at the reverend.

"Sorry, I just got carried away, but please Colin, try to let the anger go."

"Thank you, Meredith," their minister responded.

After the second session Colin asked Meredith to come back to his home. He wanted to show her all that he had accomplished since she came last.

He showed Meredith all around. She did not say a word but went from room to room, noting new paint and space gained back from removing a lot of furniture and belongings. Colin watched Meredith continue to smile as she checked things out. They returned to the living room as Meredith looked down at the floor.

"Did you recarpet; your home smells, well, nice, clean?"

"I did, living room, dining room and down the halls. I moved into my parents' room; carpet replaced there. I sure like having my own bathroom; don't have to walk down the hall now to go to the john," he chuckled.

Meredith looked up to him and nodded, "I'm glad you are giving yourself a couple of special gifts, like a close bathroom for one."

"Trying to take better care of myself, and I for sure feel better about the old homestead now. Again," Colin stumbled as he tried to talk, "th, th, thank you for believing in me."

She high fived him. They smiled to each other.

"Want to show you the barn; your dad and his brother's suggestion."

They walked from the home to the barn. Colin took her through an inside door on one side of the barn.

"This looks a lot like what my dad has, Colin."

"Should, I took his idea when he was here and went with it."

"Been getting any sleep?"

"Not a lot, been excited to get things fixed up; to get the place in order so I can concentrate on the corn crop."

"How's it looking?"

"Fine, I am real happy with the fields. I've let that fear go over the corn failing."

"Crop insurance?"

"Oh yeah, had to."

"Good, you're covered, whether the corn makes it or not. I need to head out, work tomorrow."

"Hey, Meredith, check it out,"

Colin opened closet doors after they returned to the house. Meredith saw a stack of over a dozen photo albums.

"I'm even working on the photo project, thanks, that was just a super idea, the video."

"That's good, your kids will need to know who your folks were, a video will certainly help."

"Right, goodnight Meredith, thanks for coming to counseling with me and for coming here. I'll try the next session by myself. See, you see, I am really trying, and I feel accomplishment."

He stopped for a second, then added, "Not anger."

Meredith watched his expression, a happier look, she decided.

"Good for you, Colin," Meredith's eyes shone into his, "the sessions helped me, Colin, did help."

"Meredith, may I call you for a date; I really want to get to know you better."

Meredith's eyes widened. Colin watched the surprised look on her face.

"I, I, yes, a date, that would be real special."

ℂ

"Meredith, I know you really want to get going on your project to take excess flowers to the hospital and to assisted living. So Phyllis and I talked. She appreciated your comments about flower waste, that the waste might be put to use."

Meredith stood with Dena as they put together some of the flower arrangements for the wedding coming up Saturday.

"And, what did she and you decide?"

"Until school starts and we have a chance to ask high school seniors about this volunteer project, Phyllis wants you to take two hours in the morning once a week to prepare and deliver flowers yourself, using the van. She's paying you for the effort, your regular hourly rate. And I'll cover the shop while you're gone."

Meredith smiled and clapped her hands.

"Oh wow, and it's fabulous advertising for us, Dena, our card on the flowers, letting the administration at both facilities know this is a volunteer effort. I consider it like a stewardship commitment to our community."

"You're right, Meredith, it's a tiny public service we want to do. Golly, I know the older folks in the nursing home love to get flowers from family and friends. I see their eyes light up 'cause sometimes the front desk lets me bring the vase of flowers to their rooms; they ask to smell them, even the folks who have a hard time. Most want the flowers nearby, so they can see them."

"Ah, flowers, sometimes soothe both the body and the soul."

Dena nodded to Meredith. Meredith watched a smile broaden her tan face with her sparkling brown eyes and dark hair.

"So it's settled."

"OK, Dena, it's tomorrow then, if it's OK with you, 'cause we've got some excess that I'll fix up before I leave tonight."

Єᴓ

Meredith held the box with four flower-filled vases and smiled as she met the assisted living administrator.

"As promised, we want to share our excess flowers with your patients. They'll just be thrown away, otherwise. You decide who gets them."

Mrs. Hawthorne smiled to Meredith.

"What a grand idea; The Flower Shop is just such a special business and we thank you. We'll save the vases for return to you, so we can keep this effort going."

Meredith left the flowers and took her box with her. She asked for permission to go out to the middle courtyard area to see the flowers the residents planted and tended. Meredith noted some of the roses, glorious reds and oranges, even an almost purple hue to one rose. At home her dad wanted only a xeriscape sort of lawn in the front yard, with just a small amount of grass. So her yard had only green shrubbery mixed with tan bushes. The yardwork at home belonged to Conner.

Then she remembered Colin's yard, neglected, full of weeds. Once Mrs. Sanderson raised beautiful roses. Meredith recalled her mom bringing home a color burst of roses from a visit she had at the Sandersons. The roses still grew in the front and to the sides of the Sanderson yard, but they were overgrown with weeds. Meredith wondered how they even stayed alive. She thought, "Cole must have remembered to water them, on top of everything else he had to do."

ೲ

Colin asked Meredith out, a real date. They saw a movie together at a theater and stopped at a coffee shop for chocolate fudge sundaes after. Meredith enjoyed her time with Colin; they talked about their futures and avoided what was going on right at the moment in their lives.

"How far did you say you wanted to go in your military career?"

"Colin, four years, the Air Force wants at least that from its officers. That will get me to Captain. That's my goal, Captain."

"Captain Raymer, ma'am, that sounds very cool. I like that."

Meredith asked him about his yard.

"Pretty sad, it's a wonder the roses survive."

"I'd like to help, maybe, try to save the roses."

Colin gave her a surprised look. Meredith watched his eyes widen and his eyebrows raise.

She related about the time her mom brought home beautiful roses from Colin's mom's garden.

"How you gonna have time to do that, with all you have to do, Missy?"

Meredith shot off her best southern drawl, "Sonny, I got every other Saturday afternoon off. That's when I would do it. I'll get info about where to trim the roses, what to use for plant food, y'all."

Colin nodded his head to her and gave Meredith a big smile.

"It'll be fun, something I can do. You know the roses could be living representatives of the folks you lost, something for you to remember them by."

Colin sat very still after he heard what Meredith suggested. His memory of the roses swept through his mind. He only remembered the neglect. Meredith watched him tear up.

"He's remembering those he's lost," Meredith thought. She got misty herself, then thought of a rose bush in her own back yard that might represent her mom.

"Sweet, oh Meredith, that's such a good idea, go for it. I'll give the yard a quick mow before you come over; it'll help sort out the weeds from the grass. I bet there's some rose food floating around; I'll look for it and leave it out for when you decide to weed the roses. Don't know what my mom's secret was to the beautiful flowers."

℘

Meredith and Conner got home from their outing. Earlier she took him to the lake where they swam and picnicked. Conner got this Sunday off; someone wanted to trade a day off with him at the store. So brother and sister took advantage of their time together. Meredith took her French horn and played it for Conner while he swam in the lake. She memorized a few pieces in high school and still remembered them. Playing the horn brought her a sense of peace, as she watched the lazy wind send a slight shimmer way out in the water.

Mr. Parker phoned Meredith. He asked her to play with the Porttown Symphony for as long as she was back home. She told him she needed to check with her dad. The symphony practiced one evening during the week for three hours.

"I think you should do it, Meredith, if you feel you have time. It's a marvelous opportunity. Don't want to sound like a nag, but hope you are taking time for yourself," Jack looked across to her at the dinner table that night.

"Dad, yes, I'm taking time for myself. Remember I don't have to study every second. I'm in great shape with my correspondence class, like nearly a third of the way through it and it's still August. I'll be OK coming home after 10 p.m. I know you don't want me to be out alone later in the evening."

"When do you have practice?"

"Tomorrow evening, it's one practice a week, I'll be here for two symphony performances, one in October and the other before the holidays."

"Are you starting to get anxious about returning to State?"

Jack watched a smile broaden across her daughter's face, "I am, but right now I'm liking living here, with my class, now the symphony, spending time with Colin and Tyler, I'm happy, fulfilled."

"That's good."

"My selfishness, the me, me, me that was such a part of me clear through my first semester at State, that's going away. I like helping out, helping others outside my own family. It's such a trip to take flowers to the folks in the home and in the hospital."

Jack smiled to her and nodded his head.

5

"Meredith Raymer, is that you?" the model good-looking young man asked.

"Wow, I don't remember him," flashed through her mind.

"Well, hi," she looked over to him as she carried her horn case down the steps from the stage.

He watched Meredith's face flare a beet red, "She doesn't know who I am," he realized.

Meredith stopped, deciding to own up to her memory lapse.

"I, I, guess I don't recall who you are."

"Meredith, I sat behind you in Calc II."

"Lucas, is that you?"

He smiled down to her, "Yeah, while you ate up the AP classes at Porttown High and then away at University, I grew up, no more pimply face, got my hair cut, and wear contacts. I'm a senior this year."

"You gained, maybe 25 pounds and added, what four inches to your height. 'Bout the only thing I recall is the voice, and the wonderful sounds of your bassoon," she commented to Lucas as she looked him up and down.

"How's State?"

"Fabulous, you know why I'm home 'til winter?"

"I do; you're helping out, now that your mom lives in California. Your folks, they're good people."

Meredith watched him smile and nod to her.

"They're divorcing."

Lucas's eyes dimmed and his lips took on a thin line, "Oh Meredith," he paused, "I am so sorry. I wondered about that."

Meredith nodded up to him, "Yeah, it sucks, such bad news for my brother and me, too."

She decided not to relate what she'd told Tyler back at State about her suspicions surrounding her mom and her wanting out for a long time.

"Want to hang out with me for a coke and fries at the high school hangout?"

"Sorry Lucas, can't. Have to get home. Dad doesn't allow me out too late by myself."

They stood in front of her car in the high school parking lot.

"How long have you been with the Symphony?"

"A year now, Mr. Parker, he's somethin', I'm in band too. I wrestle in the winter and run spring track. But hey, I'm doin' what I love, working at Doc Monroe's veterinary practice. I'm kinda a tech there; been working for him for three years. I love the animals. Once in a while he takes me on a house call with him, to take care of the big sick guys."

"So your passion is taking care of sick animals?"

"Right, I'm applying to both Iowa State and Kansas State soon. My supreme desire is to be a vet, what's yours?"

"Studying chemistry at K State; I want to be a chemist. I'm also working to commission as an officer in the Air Force. I want a job when I graduate. Hey, I gotta go."

"Can I call you sometime; I'd like to go out with you."

Meredith looked over to him and smiled, "OK, we're in the phone book like the family's been for the last 40 years, yeah it'd be fun to go out."

"Take care, Meredith, it's so good to see you again, you're more beautiful than I remember."

Meredith saw a sincere look in his eyes and in his voice as he said that to her.

"See ya, Lucas."

℘

"OK Meredith, the more boys you get to know, the better idea you'll have later on about what you want in a man. Enjoy yourself, now while you don't have to study all the time," she said out loud as she drove out to her farm. The quiet at home made her conscious her dad and Conner turned in early. Everyone had stuff going on the next day. But she had just a half day of work, Saturday, no wedding.

℘

Colin did what he said he would. He mowed the front and side yards of the Sanderson home. He went over the lawn a second time, with the grass catcher. The first time he had to rake up bag after bag of tall grass. Meredith figured that out when she saw the bags of grass out by the trash as she drove up. Meredith found a note taped on the front door.

Thank you Meredith for helping out with the roses, which helps me. The yard-a terrible mess, but better now that I mowed. I left you clippers, rose food, aphid spray for after you water, and bags. I've decided, I think I talked to you about swimming in sorrow. Yeah, I was then. Now, I feel like I got an anchor, you, when grief starts to get me. I climb up that anchor, thinking of you, I start to feel better. I'm rambling. Go to it! Love, Colin

Meredith eyed the whole area.

"This place, the yard and the house, sure are prettier than ours." She shook her head, "Pure neglect, I'll bet I can find some blooming roses among all the weeds and thorns," she challenged herself.

Two hours later Meredith approached the last area, the side yard, with the fewest roses next to the home. She couldn't believe the difference pulling a few thousand weeds would make. She took off her gloves and plopped in the grass to drink the iced coffee from her thermos. Meredith remembered to wear long sleeves. But her lower arms and hands had little bloody pricks all over them.

She donned her gloves again and dug into the roses. She developed a routine that worked well, in routing out the weeds. She snipped off the dead heads from previous flowers. And in a few cases she cut off dead branches of the roses.

"Time for rose food, and water," she said to the rose bushes. "Mrs. Sanderson, if you're looking down, your roses are beautiful again. Maybe Colin will get to like the idea of remembering his family through these remarkable growing plants. I hope so," she spoke out.

She applied the rose food and spent time watering each plant. She put the clippers and rose food back on the porch and wound up the hose where she found it. She finished off spraying all the plants with the aphid spray.

"Unbelievable, I needed five bags to deal with this mess," she thought. She carefully removed the bags to the back trash, knowing there were small rose prickles to catch her gloved hands and covered arms and legs.

Before she got in her car, she walked through the yard again, eyeing each rose bush that she just tended.

"I'll take just one rose. I want Colin to see that almost every rose plant has at least one rose blooming. Ah, everything," she paused and then spoke out again, "looks so nice, good job."

She stood in the front yard for a bit longer.

"I helped; I like that. I had no idea I would enjoy flowers, like here, and also at the shop, so much. Maybe Colin will pick a bush in memory, maybe for his mom at least?" she asked herself.

She nodded her head in wonder as she smelled the tangy odor of the rose she picked to take home.

That night after dinner she asked Conner to come out with her to their small backyard. She watched tall corn plants wave to them in the easy breeze. They walked to the small grouping of roses her mother tended since as far back as they could remember.

"Conner, you done a good job keeping the roses weeded."

"Thanks, Mere," he smiled as he looked at her. "Dad helped me figure out what to put on the roses for fertilizer."

"I want to pick a rose bush to remember mom by."

Conner reached up to hold onto her shoulder, "Maybe I won't be so sad if I have somethin' real right here at home to look at, to help me with mom. Mere, what about, what do you think about the pretty yellow and pink rose bush? The colors remind me of mom; she didn't say much but she smiled, especially to you and me."

"That's it, Conner. You and me, her sunny smile, I'll call this bush Mom Julie. What'cha think?"

Meredith turned to him and leaned to hug him.

"I like that, Mere. Does dad need to know?"

"He doesn't, it's our special remembering of mom, OK?"

Meredith felt tears forming in her eyes. That caused Conner to cry. They held each other for a little while. Conner remembered clippers. They cut one rose from Mom Julie bush, and roses from three other bushes to bring inside for a bouquet.

Ⅎ

When they met with their counselor the next time Conner explained what they decided to do for a remembrance of their mom. He smiled as he talked. Meredith felt a huge welling of pride, goose bumpy, for her brother as they left the meeting. They held hands as they walked to Meredith's car.

"That was awesome, Conner, how you told about Mom Julie. I am very proud of you," she said as she looked at him.

She saw something she hadn't seen in Conner for a while. She saw his happy eyes.

෨

Colin called Meredith and invited her to go dancing. He thanked her for weeding the rose bushes. That same evening she got a short note from Tyler. For that fall semester he accepted the duties of detachment cadet commander. He needed to get his car back to Manhattan to meet with his cadet staff. They had to plan for new cadet orientation. Meredith did not hear from Tyler for some time. She felt sure he dated other women that summer, just as she went out with Colin. It was a boundary she agreed to accept. The next day Lucas called and asked her out. She accepted a date with him.

෨

Meredith's head spun. In the past two weeks she dated Colin twice and Lucas twice. She started making comparisons. But there really weren't any. Lucas was a year older than her, still in high school. And despite his intelligence and his abilities and his future goals, he still had an immaturity Meredith knew she was past. Life had not handed him difficulties yet. Could he cope? Meredith accepted that she could handle life now, but a year ago, she was just a spoiled kid who had everything handed to her, a car, and a college education. Through being with Lucas, Meredith could see how much she matured.

Colin, however, was six years older. And life dealt him a heavy hand, especially since he graduated from State. His struggles were like hers, fear of failing, at the farm, for him, and fear of a poor performance at the flower shop and fear of letting her family down, for Meredith.

On their last date Colin and Meredith talked about how she could get her dad, Conner, and Uncle Milt prepared for her leaving for good, for the University and for her Air Force career. They decided it had to be gradual, small stuff first. Colin suggested laundry be the first item. All three men knew how to run a washer and dryer, piece of cake compared to the fancy farm equipment they drove with ease.

"I hate laundry, Meredith. I don't do it until it's piled sky high. Then I cuss myself for waiting so long, 'cause the stuff I need is wet."

"So it'll sort of be trial and error, right?"

"Yeah, be sure you let your guys know you aren't doing their sheets or their towels; they need to include those things when they do their wash. Geez, Meredith, I remember some pretty stinky sheets until I got in gear and remembered everything that needed washing."

"How long did it take you to get in the washing and drying groove?"

Colin shook his head and gave her a disgusted look, "Two months, but I got things under control, finally."

"What after that?"

"Let's see, vacuuming, nah, I doubt if they'll ever dust."

"Conner might, he keeps his room real neat."

"Oh, yeah, everybody vacuums their own room, and yeah, bathrooms, I'd assign those, your dad's bathroom to your dad, and Conner's bathroom to him. Bathrooms are the worst."

He pointed his finger down his throat.

"Yeah, 'cause you guys don't always aim straight," Meredith remembered a couple of messes and started laughing.

"I guess if your guys have to clean up their own messy urine, they'll eventually get their act straight, right?"

Meredith laughed and laughed at Colin's comment.

She nodded to him, "That'll be about the only way."

"So," Meredith watched his cute smile, "what'll you do around the house after you give away all your chores?"

"The cooking, yeah, I will need to give my guys a few lessons about cooking roasts. Everyone at my house is a meat and potato person. Conner remembers quite a bit from his times helping me when I took over."

"Meredith, you would be proud of me, I do steak, pork chops, chicken breasts, salmon just real good. I watched mom back in the day. She was a very good cook."

"So was mine," Meredith nodded to him.

Meredith and Colin ordered dessert at the cozy restaurant where they ate dinner.

"Colin, I want to ask you about somethin' that's bothered me since I was knee high, and one of the reasons I'm studying chemistry."

"Shoot."

She shook her head, then paused, "Where to begin?"

"Just start," Colin waited, his eyes steady upon her face.

She looked at him, "My grandparents died way young, really sick, dad took over at 17. Your dad, died of cancer, your mom, dementia, they were way young so you and Cole took over, very young. I been taking a mental inventory of the farm families around the area. And I've noticed somethin' pretty disturbing, plus the retardedness in my own family, Uncle Milt, and Conner."

Colin nodded his head and took her hand in his.

"I also paid attention to what's goin' on in our families. It's scary, 'cause they're some brain tumors and other pretty bad cancers that folks have around here."

"The pesticides that were once used?" Meredith raised her eyebrow in question.

"Yeah, pretty sure, that's in our bodies, genetics, from previous generations who lived with the really nasty pesticides."

"Our water?"

"Yeah, from our wells, I imagine stuff in our aquifer, too."

"I would love to be able to test water samples from a couple of our wells."

"You may not like what you find out; Cole said to leave that whole deal the hell alone. He figured if we weren't sick by now, that we escaped it."

"But what about for our kids, don't you think they deserve a better shake at this?"

Colin squeezed her hand and let go.

"I gotta ponder that, but I want to have our water tested from a couple different wells. That is an outstanding suggestion, Meredith. I wonder if anybody in the family ever even thought about that?"

"I doubt it," Meredith shook her head to him, "they had enough trouble just livin' day to day. It was a rough life, not that long ago."

She looked above Colin's head, envisioning plowing the ground with the power of a horse.

"And for heaven's sakes, bringing in the corn at harvest, what a huge chore, with a horse and wagon and people's hands."

"You're right, Meredith, we are blessed beyond measure to have our technology."

That night Colin walked Meredith to her door. They kissed, their first kiss. A deep heat hit Meredith's groin. She felt it, like a hot ember inside her. Colin kissed her again, exploring her whole mouth. They stepped back from each other. Hunger held in each set of eyes, Meredith saw it, and so did Colin. Meredith raised her arms and came into a hug with him.

"Oh Meredith, oh," he paused, "wow," as he whispered in her ear.

They parted as they smiled to each other. Meredith waited on the porch until she saw his wave. She let herself in.

೮౧

Meredith lay in bed, but she did not sleep. She liked her friendship with Colin. She knew she was helping him, and she knew he appreciated her help. He was finding himself, believing in his ability to get through the pain, fear, sadness he felt. And there was more, Meredith felt love for him, more than what God said, "To love one another." Her feelings for him felt both gentle and sexual.

"I cannot commit, to anyone, not now, and not for a very long time," she said it out loud, one, two, three times. "And I have feelings for Tyler too. Meredith, don't get yourself in a dating mess, hear girl? More than one guy, well now I'm seeing two, and Tyler makes three, but when will I see him again?" That question remained on her mind as she went to sleep.

೮౧

Near the end of August Jack Raymer attended church with Meredith. He attended with her for a few weeks now. Meredith liked his being with her. After service they went in to the fellowship time for coffee and conversation with members of the congregation. After the third week of this routine Meredith began to pay attention to her dad. They both circulated among the group. The last couple of times Jack Raymer stopped to chat with a newcomer to the congregation. Her dad mentioned to Meredith that the lady was a new teacher at Porttown High, and that she was not married or in a relationship now.

"Dad, I haven't asked you," Meredith looked over to him as they left the fellowship hall, "but I gotta ask now, is your divorce final?"

"It is; it happened quick, uncontested, both your mom and I are single people again. Doggone strange, don't know how to get used to it. Don't think I'm ready to date anyone."

Meredith watched her dad's face as he drove home. He seemed more pleasant lately, and it showed in the look on his face, his clearer eyes. He turned to her and smiled, "I need to get to know women in a friendship sort of way. I admire you, Meredith, you have three guy friends, all different, that you enjoy. Tyler, you can't be with him, but he'll be someone for you back at school next year. And Lucas and Colin, they're about as different from each other as it's possible to be. Lucas seems lots more comfortable with you, maybe because you two are close in age. Let me see, he's a year older than you, right?"

"That's right, but I have to tell you, I'm a heck of a lot more mature than he is."

Jack chuckled to her, "OK, sweet pea, I'll take your word for that," he paused, "right, you've lived a lot of life and disappointment, tragedy, too since you got home in June."

ℰℐ

Meredith recalled Colin's prediction about the laundry chore at the Raymer house. The men did not like it. Conner helped Meredith with laundry when he was younger. So he led out for the men, but messed up putting too much soap in with his wash. He had to rewash two loads with no soap in them to get his clothes back in condition. Conner also dried his clothes for too long. Everything came out wrinkly. His clothes got washed three times and dried twice before he got the hang of it. He told his dad and Uncle Milt about his problems in the hope they would not have the same thing happen to them.

It took about three weeks, but Meredith's hopeless men and their wash did get better.

At dinner one evening in early September Meredith looked around the table, "Looks like you all have got laundry squared away, so it's time to divide up the bare floor cleanup and carpet vacuuming. Uncle Milt, you're got your own place, but Dad, you and Conner need to divide up the house."

Discussion ensued. No one was happy.

"I can see, fellas," she paused and looked from one disgruntled face to the next, "that taking me out of the housework equation is going to be harder than I thought."

She heard a lot of grumbling, but the men worked out their assigned tasks. Meredith stood by for the first couple of times Conner and Jack did their floor and vacuum chores. By the third time they did a job of which Meredith approved.

Meredith thanked them for their efforts, but added, "You all run a big corn operation, seems like with little trouble, but you dang well are having a hard time with this little old house."

They nodded their heads to her, "You're right," Jack mumbled.

℘

Colin asked Meredith to a Porttown High football game. After they went to a bar which served up delicious snacks. Colin ordered a beer for him, pop for Meredith and chicken wings for them both.

"Well, did you have a chance to reminisce, Colin?"

"I did, it was fun. You mentioned a lot of people you hadn't seen for quite a while. Do you miss the crowd from high school?"

"Nah, I always was thinkin' so far ahead, to college; I much prefer college students. They're capable of great discussions, not just who took who to what thing here, who's seeing who, that's what high school is."

"Meredith, where did your wanting to be in the military come from?"

"Yeah, I get asked that. Nobody in my family served. They stayed back on the farm. I want to serve, plain and simple. My brother can't, but I will step up and do it, my patriotic duty."

"That makes sense, it's just another way that I admire the heck out of you. You know what you want. You know how to go after it."

"But, once again, Colin," she shook her head, "I'm struggling, at home, at work, I want to get back to school, I don't want to wait 'til January. My patience is starting to wear thin with my family. They are very capable of running a home. My housekeeping standards are definitely not theirs. And that's OK. I gotta step back but still help some, especially with the upcoming corn harvest which will take October for dad."

"Meredith, he's been doing the harvest all his life. He'll handle it, just like you told me, believe in your family, you must take care of yourself, that's so important," Colin touched Meredith's cheek. He watched her break into a smile at his comment.

Meredith stopped the smile, pursed her lips together in a thin line, and shook her head, "I sure as hell hope dad can handle it all."

Colin could not help it. He broke into a laugh at the tone of her voice as she made that comment.

₭

Lucas walked Meredith to her car after symphony practice. Mr. Parker held an abbreviated practice because of another commitment he had.

"I'm happy as heck with how the symphony is getting along; we play good stuff, don't you think?" Lucas asked.

"Yeah, going good, whow and I can't believe Mr. Parker's gonna let us do *There You'll Be.*"

Lucas looked over to her, "Yeah I totally agree, what a love song, right?"

She nodded.

Meredith," he stopped her and put a hand on her upper arm, "come with me to the lake Saturday night; music, dancing, a little al-co-hol on the beach."

"Geez, Lucas, are you guys all crazy?" She lowered her voice and leaned against her car. She put her horn case on the ground. "You know Sheriff Banyon. Somebody'll snitch or open their fat traps and talk; he'll have his deputies on the road after the party, a sobriety check point, and the whole mess of you'll get stopped, the cops will smell your stinkin' alcohol breaths. You'll get picked up for underage drinking and driving while intoxicated. Lucas, the sheriff will not put up with crap. You know he runs an extremely tight county. Folks have to go to a different county to party; the law there's not so," she paused, "well, you know. No way, the sheriff doesn't want any football players suspended from the team. So there better not be football players at the party. And second of all you know what the football coach wants, the same thing the sheriff wants, winning sports teams. Don't do it, Lucas. You could lose your license. Then how will you get to doc to help out with the animals?"

By that time Meredith's face flushed; she saw the consequences so clear in her head. She thought about alcohol consumption herself. Then she remembered about the colonel at her detachment at State. All matters of the law, no matter how small, a speeding ticket, anything that a cadet did, had to be reported to him. She wouldn't drink, not now, until she was of age, a long time away. Colonel Redmore removed cadets from the program, cadets who broke laws. She had her dream for her future.

"Nope, Lucas, I won't go with you; sorry, my future is too important to me."

Lucas hugged her and watched her drive away.

ℰℴ

Dena took a week off for vacation. Meredith handled a wedding and a funeral by herself. Phyllis checked in, but Meredith said she could take care of everything. At dinner Saturday night Meredith told about her week.

"I don't ever want to have to take on a business by myself. I am going to insist that Phyllis start looking for help. There is a lot of training that goes into running a place like the shop."

"Mere, sorta do you know how dad feels, running a big operation like this?"

"Conner, I'm starting too," she looked from her dad to her uncle and then at her brother. "I guess it's the big dump of responsibility that I don't like. What if I screw up, man, I don't want to fail, at anything."

She watched her dad smile to her, "The shop survived the week, right?"

Meredith nodded to him.

"Well all right then, nice job, sweet pea."

Meredith felt good about his comment. Some of her confidence returned as she prepared for the next week at work.

"I'm OK, right?" she looked in her bathroom mirror as she brushed her teeth. Her mind flew ahead, a busy week, Porttown's Homecoming, always early, before the corn harvest.

6

"Uncle Milt, hi, is everything OK? You never call me at the shop."

There was a pause.

"Uncle Milt?"

"Oh, Meredith, need your help. I'm with your dad; we're at the hospital. He's been admitted. I need for you to pick up Conner. I called the store; they'll let him go early."

"Uncle Milt, what's going on?"

"Remember, your dad talked to us about taking down the one small run-down outbuilding we've got on the place. You know how he likes everything nice and neat."

"What happened?"

"Well, he knocked down the sides with a sledge hammer. One of the corners, somehow collapsed on him, landed on his left arm and leg. And a board gashed him on the side of the head. It's a miracle the roof didn't come down on him."

"The roof?"

"Yeah, Meredith, he should a taken the roof off first, but he wanted to do the job quick. So this happened."

"Did you call 911?"

"Course, they came double quick. I was heading out to help him when I heard him screamin' at the top of his lungs. I sure had to pull a lot of lumber off him."

"That was so good that you were there, Uncle Milt. Otherwise he could'a laid there for a long time. I'll finish up here and go pick up Conner. We'll see you and dad at the hospital."

℘

Uncle Milt, Meredith and Conner stood around Jack Raymer's hospital bed.

"I'm a stupid shit; I don't know why I just didn't take the little tractor and ram into the little place. Instead, I had to be the big man and flex my muscles with the sledge hammer. Look where it got me."

Jack smiled to his family. Meredith started to giggle, it caught Conner up, and Uncle Milt joined in. The three of them pointed to Jack, and they all laughed together.

"Gosh damn, I know better," her dad said, after they finished laughing. "I gotta stay overnight. They want to check my head in the morning, probably a concussion. You see the stitches. Do you think the hit on my head might knock some sense into me?" he asked looking from one person to the other.

All three visitors shook their heads and spoke out together, an emphatic, "No."

Jack shook his head after he watched them shake theirs, "Figured that's what you all would say."

"Dad, this is the voice of reason, what's the deal with your arm and leg?"

"Thanks sweet pea, for getting us back on track, left ankle is sprained; the collapse broke a couple bones in my foot. Be in a boot for my foot and ankle."

He held up his left wrist, showed them the cast, "broken."

The three of them watched Jack. His forehead wrinkled and he looked from one to the other.

"Sure gonna need your help with harvest. Conner, if you can get some time off, and Meredith, please see if you can reduce your hours. Didn't you say the shop was bringing someone else on to replace you before Christmas time?"

"That's right, Dad, we'll help out, we'll get through this. I know Colin will help us when he's not harvesting, and our neighbors, they'll pitch in, just like you've done for them in the past."

"The worst, guys, crap, I'm left handed. I'm so left handed I can't do much of anything with my right hand."

"You'll learn," the three of them said in unison to Jack.

෨

Meredith worked a half day and took the afternoon to help Uncle Milt at home. Her dad hobbled around the Raymer house. He kept a crutch under his right arm and walked very lightly on his left ankle, putting most of his weight on his right leg.

"No way am I taking that strong pain medicine, it makes me so flippin' oozy," he said to Meredith.

"You look like you just got the livin' crap beat out of you, Dad," Meredith looked him in the eye as she got him to sit down in a comfortable chair in the living room.

"You're not making me feel any better, Meredith," he said, his voice now weary.

"Dad, these are not prescription but you'll need two for the pain."

Jack said not a word but swallowed the pills and drank the glass of water Meredith brought to him. He pushed the chair to a bit of a recline. Meredith felt his cool forehead.

"Good, no infection," she said to herself as she watched his eyes close.

৯১

Later Colin called Meredith.

"Several farm families share the harvesting equipment. I'll find out where it's housed this year and make sure all the maintenance's been done. That way we'll be ready to roll when the corn says it's time."

"Thanks, Colin."

"Who's responsible for the scheduling?"

"The corn, Meredith, it's always nuts 'cause the equipment is usually needed on two fields at the same time. And I haven't done the actual harvest in four years, bein' at school. So Don Prescott, I think you know him, he's my neighbor back of our place, he'll figure out about the timing. He's been doing it for a long time now. I have every confidence in him."

"Well, I'm sure Uncle Milt remembers how this all works. He'll be our main guide for the Raymer farm, responsible for the physical efforts."

"Meredith, it's all gonna work out. I'll need your dad to advise me, as this is all happening, at my place like at yours. He's the brains, and we all can be the brawn."

৯১

"Unbelievable, what a week," Meredith shook her head to Dena. It was the Thursday before Homecoming. "I guess I've never seen so many big yellow mums before in my life."

"Meredith, you sorta missed out, zooming through high school at such a young age. Homecoming is a pretty big deal in our town, the parade, the Friday night bonfire, the Saturday afternoon game, and the dance. We do flowers for the game and for the dance. Having a good football team for most of the years I've been around is a big draw. It gets alums back here for the weekend. We're lucky to have excellent teachers, who stay awhile, so the alums come back to see them as well as their old classmates. Porttown High is a fine school."

"Gosh, I'm glad you think so; I flew through so fast, I guess I didn't take the time." Meredith stopped, letting her high school years swirl through her memory. Dena watched Meredith's smile and nod, "to see that it was a good school. I'll for sure see a couple of my teachers when I go to the game. And Mr. Parker, oh, do you know I'm filling in temporary in the horn section of our local symphony?"

"Nope, I didn't know that, you mentioned you help your church choir."

"Got the time, don't have to study much for my correspondence class. It's easy-smeezy compared to good old chemistry. Dena, have you asked Phyllis yet about hiring on someone to replace me before long?"

"I have," Dena shook her head to Meredith. Meredith watched Dena's face change to a serious look. "She doesn't want to even think about it. But I told her I could not handle the shop by myself, she'd either have to get someone or come back to work pretty much full time."

"You are staying on, right Dena?"

"I won't be, unless I get a raise. I love the work, but I got bills to pay. So I guess we're in a wait and see mode. Thank goodness you're here, Meredith."

Dena stopped what she was doing, came around and gave Meredith a hug.

"Where ever you end up, babe, those folks'll be lucky to have you. You ever need a reference, I'll do one for you, OK?"

They released their hug. Dena watched Meredith tear up.

"Thank you, Dena."

"Hey, I think we've got a high school senior to take over as a volunteer."

"To deliver flowers to the hospital and assisted living facility?"

"Yeah, Phyllis contacted the lead counselor at Porttown High. That counselor helps kids with volunteering and employment when requests come in. Two girls expressed an interest. Phyllis says you went to school with them, a few years ago, before you started accelerating your program to the university."

"That's great, Dena I gotta transition out of here, we've just got October and November."

"Hey, you'll stay on 'til Christmas?"

Meredith shook her head. She watched Dena's expression, her mouth solemn and her dark eyes, not happy.

"I'm not sure, depends on dad."

≈

Jack Raymer struggled; he never had a broken bone before, even though he played high school football and kept active on the farm since he was out of diapers.

"I hate that I have to wear a cover around my wrist when I shower. Damn, I can hardly get the cover on with my stupid right hand."

Jack had a litany of other complaints that the rest of the family ignored. Jeepers often sat close to him when Jack took his rests, which were every late morning and mid-afternoon.

He insisted on attending church with Meredith, and the coffee after became critical for him. He spent more and more time each week chatting with the teacher who caught his eye weeks before. Meredith also introduced herself to Jessica Anton a few weeks before. They greeted each other after Jack and Jessica talked for a bit.

"Meredith, I brought something for all of you at the farm. Your dad told me he loved chocolate chips bars. I made some. He seems fit to be tied with his injuries, sure can tell he's not used to be sick."

"He's been an absolute pill about his whole situation. He and Uncle Milt get into a shouting match about once a day."

Meredith shook her head and smiled to Jessica.

"The corn will be harvested, one way or another. The harvest is dad's great big baby, this time he won't have all the say."

Jessica laughed, "He's calmer with me; he's tried to make sense of what happened to him."

Meredith looked her in the eye, "Sometimes Dad just blasts ahead, without thinking stuff through. But," she nodded, "he's healing and that's the best thing."

Meredith walked with Jessica to get the tray of chocolate chip bars where she placed her wrap and purse.

"Thank you, Jessica, the real way to my dad's heart is through the old tummy."

They nodded their heads to each other.

"Oh, Meredith, please call me Jess, OK?"

Meredith acknowledged her with a "See ya, Jess. We'll all sure enjoy these," she looked down at the goodies she held in her hands

She searched to find her dad. Meredith saw him limp out of the fellowship hall.

"He's standing up straighter and the limp, it's better," she thought to herself.

When they got to Meredith's car, Jack noticed the package she carried.

"What's that?"

"Chocolate chip bars, Jess made them for us."

Jack smiled to his daughter, "Well, I'll be."

"Want to tell me about her, Dad?

"Well, we talk by phone; I like to hear her voice."

Meredith kept her mouth shut for as long as she could. As she turned into the lane of the farm, she just blurted it out.

"Rebound, Dad, take it easy. Have you ever dated anybody besides mom?" She turned her gaze to her dad and watched him turn his eyes to her.

"Not really. And my counselor and I already talked about rebound, Jess knows too. She's helping with a foster child, living with Jess, a girl two years younger than you."

"Do you know the foster story?"

"Yeah, very messed-up situation."

"Have you met the girl?"

"Yeah, she's quiet, Jess's done a super job with the girl's appearance, and helping the girl understand that some people do care. I c'n sorta feel the girl's really suffered, never seen her smile. You got me spoiled, sweet pea, doggone, you're so advanced for your age. I kinda compare the little gal with Conner. He's a kind guy, and I bet they would like each other."

"Dad, what's her name?"

"Hailee."

When they got in their home, Jack limped to the kitchen table with his coffee.

"Meredith, gonna tell me about Homecoming, the dance with Colin?"

"Yesterday was great, we won the game, we've got such a good football team, and the dance, oh my gosh, Dad, Colin and I talked with people I remember from school. He loves to dance, just like I do."

Meredith left it at that. But when she went to her room and changed, she felt the tears burning her eyes. She sat on the floor and recalled the situation out on the dance floor last night. She and Colin rocked together in a beautiful slow dance.

"I found it, Meredith."

"What's that, Colin?"

"My family rose, it's out front, a bright sunny yellow, helps me remember, especially my mom, but dad too, and Cole. It makes me feel better when I see the blooms."

"That's so good. Conner and I picked a rose bush in our back yard, for our mom."

"Julie?"

"Yeah, the rose is both pinkish and yellowish, makes us remember her smile."

After the dance ended, Meredith's eyes looked up to his.

"What'll you do in the winter, when the snow's on everything, Colin?"

"When I want to, I'll buy roses."

"Colin, my rose for mom, it's there in my memory, it'll stay there."

Later they danced to another slow melody. Colin smelled her hair and her light flowery perfume as he held her close.

"Remember this, remember her," he told his brain.

He bent his head down and whispered in her ear.

"Meredith, I love you. One day I want you to be my wife."

Meredith felt a sexual jolt that started in her groin and moved up and up until her forehead felt on fire. She moved her head from the curve of his neck and looked up into his eyes.

"Friendship, Colin, I love our friendship, you, are, my best friend, but that's what it is, our friendship."

She remained calm and solemn as she continued to look up at him.

He blinked several times, "I guess I know that, Meredith."

They returned to their slow dance.

Colin walked her to the Raymer front porch after the dance.

Meredith heard the waver in his voice, "Cuh, c'n I still continue to see you?"

Colin watched her smile broaden as she nodded her head. That was enough.

"Harvest's coming," Colin said.

"We're ready,"

∽

Meredith shook out of her reverie about the dance the night before. She knew what she needed to do. And she had a plan for a while. She continued to work it out in her head as she prepared flowers at work. Meredith met a new teacher at Porttown High. They both played in the symphony. She played second chair violin, and she looked young to Meredith. The more she and Meredith talked before practice, the more Meredith liked her. Laura grew up on a farm in Nebraska. She always wanted to be a teacher. Before this night's practice, Laura and Meredith walked into the auditorium together.

"What about the students here?"

Laura looked over to Meredith, "Ones here, in better shape math-wise than the ones I worked with last year in Nebraska. I walked into a middle-of-the-year situation. Here I've been with the students since the start of school. I like the students at Porttown High, a lot of good kids, college material. Working with them on math excites me. And they are a challenge," she nodded her head to Meredith.

Meredith noticed that Laura kept a serious look on her face as she spoke.

"You're getting anxious, aren't you?" Laura asked as they made their way to the stage.

"Countin' those days, hey, there's someone I want you to meet, he's your age. Colin and I are friends, my best friend now, we been through a lot, big losses. But I'm leavin' and I think you'd like him."

Meredith gave Laura Colin's phone number.

"Please, just meet him, you never know," Meredith ended with her voice up in the air.

Laura laughed to her, "Hey, I'll do that, for me and for you, too."

On the way out Lucas caught up with her.

"Can I catch a ride with you, please?"

"Sure."

On the way to his home, Lucas told her what happened to him after the Saturday night drinking at the lake. His parents stopped letting him drive a car.

"You were right, Meredith, I wish I had listened to you. I am one terrifically stupid piece of shit."

Meredith looked over to him as he got out of the car. He did not look at her.

"Thanks," he said as he shut the door. Meredith drove off, not waiting for him to walk to his front door.

ℰ

Meredith completed her matchmaking effort with a phone call to Colin. They talked harvest first and then Meredith introduced the idea of meeting Laura.

She hoped she gave him enough information so he might follow through on her request.

"Colin, my wish for you, expand your friendships. You helped me. And I will forever cherish your friendship."

"After harvest, Meredith, I promise."

"I hope it's OK; I gave her your number."

ℰ

They harvested the corn. Jack reported that the corn harvester still needed to work half of their fields. Every morning he met with Milt and Colin.

"We're gonna do all your fields, too, Colin. Your corn is a bit behind ours. You're helpin' us; we'll help you."

The harvester broke down just once; the repairman had it back working in under an hour. The skies held. The farmers got word that snow might be headed their way. Everybody prayed that the temperatures would raise enough to prevent that from happening. As it happened, the snow cell missed their area completely. Other parts of the region did not luck out.

Meredith took as much time off work as she could. Phyllis kept her word and brought on a part-time helper at the flower shop. Meredith and Dena saw that it was slow going because Amber never worked in a flower shop before. Meredith and Dena learned patience after she came on board. Amber's release from jail and parole meant she had to keep her job. And, Amber's mom and Phyllis had a long-standing friendship.

ℰℴ

"Meredith, she's definitely not you," Dena commented one morning before Amber arrived. "You been in the shop for several years now, and you are so smart. This little gal's goin' to be another matter completely. I'm upping the amount of pay I want in order to stay with this little business. You, my dear have been a joy to work with."

Meredith watched the smile broaden on Dena's face.

"Thanks for that, Dena."

ℰℴ

They expressed their delight at how well Amber did as a helper to the wedding planners. That Saturday's wedding showed off both their and the bride's careful planning. The affair lasted just two and a half hours, from very short wedding ceremony to a small reception. The three Flower Shop employees enjoyed every minute of it.

Amber explained after they returned to the store with the van, "Awesome, totally, my favorite part of working here."

Meredith and Dena moved their eyes from Amber and looked at each other.

"She's gonna make it," they both thought as they watched each other nod.

ℰℴ

Meredith never forgot the last days of corn harvest. Their fields were done, all the corn collected and accounted for. The Sanderson corn harvested late. Everyone kept checking the skies. And Jack Raymer examined the kernels until he gave the harvester the go ahead. The final day of the Sanderson harvest started out sunny with blue skies. That was not the case now. A storm from the northeast was due in.

Meredith felt the tension in the air, the barometer jumping around. She began to understand why this critical time meant so much to the farmers. The weather could be their greatest friend, or their worst enemy. As it turned out the storm had a lot of wind but no rain or snow. Colin's corn came in, their part of the harvest, for the Raymer and Sanderson families, completed.

Colin joined them for dinner the night they finished.

"Unbelievable, the pressure, to get everything completed while the weather held. Guys, I, I guess I just don't remember what it was really like for you."

Jack smiled to Meredith, "That's 'cause, you weren't really in the mix of things. Now you know."

Meredith's eyes went from man to man; she nodded, "Yeah, I know."

Conner added, "And I know what's for dessert, the most important part of our day."

"Yeah, so do we," Milt, Colin and Jack answered, "cherry pie with vanilla ice cream."

Meredith baked two cherry pies. When dessert finished, only two pieces of the second pie remained.

"Your pie, Mere, awesome, thanks."

"Yeah, it was worth waiting for both harvests to be completed to eat your pie," Colin smiled to her and all the men agreed.

"Conner, I can teach you the secret to my pie, if you want to learn," Meredith explained.

"Uh huh, teach me."

Everyone laughed at Conner's exuberant comment, his face pasted with a big smile.

"I want to thank each of you, SO MUCH, for helping me with harvest." Jack's eyes went from Conner to Milt to Colin to Meredith. "Never in my life have I ever felt so frustrated as this year. I'm healing, but I just hate myself, my stupid bad, with my little demolition project. My timing's terrible."

"I also want to thank you all for helping me get my crop in. It's been a very good year for the corn, been real pleased," Colin smiled to the whole group.

Meredith heard the thankfulness in his voice and watched his smile.

"He's doing, well, super good," she told herself.

ℰ

"Go out with me, Meredith. There's a movie I want to see. I would like to see it with you. Then we could go out for sundaes."

Meredith stood in the kitchen holding the phone. Halloween neared. She worked hard at the shop and at home, some things slipping until harvest completed.

"I, I, that would be nice, Colin. I know you've been working hard, me too, so much to do after the initial harvest comes in. Yes, I accept."

The chick flick movie left Meredith feeling vulnerable. Now she cared about several guys and she realized every day that her time in Iowa slipped away. She and Colin talked about the movie as they sat together at the cozy café where they liked the sundaes.

"Thanks, Meredith," Colin smiled to her. She watched a blush rise from his shirt collar up to the top of his head.

"What, WHAT, Colin, tell me."

"Laura and I agreed to meet."

"Oh, Colin, good for you," Meredith touched his hand, "that's good, wanta share?"

"Now you're a matchmaker, Meredith. I like her; her roots are in ag too. I feel real weird taking two different women out."

"You'll never know what you really want until you get to know different women. I sure hope you have fun."

Colin's face turned solemn. Meredith watched the glint in his eyes.

"My eyes, my feelings, my heart, they belong to you, Meredith. I know, I know, I gotta date others. You and me, we're so comfortable together, best friends. It'll help, when you're gone, and I'll know that you have feelings for another."

She felt his other hand over her hand. He held on.

"I don't want to let go of you, right here, right now. I wish I could freeze this scene. I will freeze it in my mind," Colin thought.

Meredith leaned in to him, her head nearly touching his face.

She whispered, "You know I love you, Colin, but I love you enough to let you go. You gotta let me go, let me go."

Colin moved his arm and put it around Meredith's shoulder. She laid her head in the crook of his neck. They sat together, their thoughts whirling about in their heads. The noise of the customers in the café faded away from them. All Meredith heard was the beating of her heart.

Five minutes passed. Meredith raised her head away from Colin and moved a bit away from him.

"We're having Thanksgiving at the farm, Colin. I want to invite you; Tyler will be there. If Laura is in town, please invite her. She and I have become friends through symphony. Dad is asking a lady he likes, her name is Jess, she has a foster daughter in her care now, Hailee. It will be fun, with Conner and Uncle Milt, a real family affair."

Colin looked over to her, "That's what I care so much about, about you, Meredith, you always think of your family." He nodded and spoke in a soft tone, "I believe, I really believe, that there's a halo of love that surrounds you, that pulls people in, yeah, a halo of love."

Colin watched spontaneous tears wash from Meredith's eyes at what he said. She looked at him, and a fresh burst of tears washed over her face.

"Oh, Colin, I will miss you, you know that."

Colin nodded his head and touched the side of her tear-stained face with his hand.

ଛଠ

The Porttown Symphony performed to a full house in late October. They played two Halloween-themed songs during the concert. But the biggest applause came from the symphony's performance of *There You'll Be*. The audience clapped and clapped for an encore. They asked for the musicians to play *There You'll Be* again. Many people knew the words, so it became a choral with orchestra accompaniment. Lots of people stood and rocked and sang along with the symphony. Meredith left the concert with her dad, uncle, and brother. None of her family attended a performance of the symphony before.

Her dad said it best, "It was great, Meredith, thank you for being a part of the group. Guys, did you hear the French horns in their solo parts?"

"Yes," they all spoke together.

"We have another concert coming up in mid-December. The music is great, so fun to play."

"We'll be there, Meredith," her dad said.

ଛଠ

Colin watched Meredith and Laura perform at the Symphony presentation. He came with Laura. And Laura made sure that Meredith saw them together after the performance. Meredith waved to them both and gave them her best beaming smile.

"I'm so glad for them, hope it works out," she said to herself. Still, as she walked out with her family she felt a little sadness, another letting go.

Meredith did not hear from Colin again until near Thanksgiving. They finally connected about the noon

Thanksgiving dinner with the Raymers. She asked him to invite Laura if Laura stayed in town for the holiday.

"Thanks for inviting me, Meredith. Laura's plans are kinda up in the air. But I would not miss one of your meals, that's for sure."

Meredith laughed at his exuberant tone of voice.

"And yes, I know you'll ask. There will be pie, pumpkin with whipped cream."

"Yeah, that's wow, great Meredith. Oh, I snipped off all the dead heads on the rose bushes around the homestead. Some still haven't gone dormant for the winter. I thank you for your idea of remembering through a live plant."

"I do it too, for our mom."

Neither of them spoke, remembering their loved ones. After a minute, Colin spoke.

"Take care, Meredith."

"Thanks, you too, Colin."

/

Tyler called her a week before Thanksgiving. The long range forecast indicated flying weather would be good for his trip from Manhattan to Porttown on Wednesday afternoon with a return to Manhattan on Saturday afternoon. Meredith kept busy at home and at the shop. She took her final exam in her correspondence art class.

"I got my A," she exclaimed as she looked at the grade that came in the mail. Her prof reminded her that the grade would not actually post until after he turned in the grades at semester's end. She thumbed through her text, remembering the beautiful works of painting, sculpture, and pottery.

She went to her dad with her news.

"Wow, nice job Meredith."

He hugged her gingerly with his arms. He no longer had the cast on his left wrist. But now he had exercises he had to do on a daily basis to restore strength in his wrist. And his foot and ankle still bothered him if he stepped wrong. Jack kept using his cane when he got tired. Meredith stepped out of his arms. They sat together and talked over the Thanksgiving dinner.

"Dad, I remind you that I did most of the Thanksgiving dinner for the past three years. So this will be no problem; I'll get organized and ask you and Conner to help do some cutting and chopping. I'm only going to do the turkey breast this year. The rest is so much waste. Is that OK?"

Meredith watched him smile to her, "Fine, sweetie, whatever you need to do, just order us around."

"Thanks, Dad, you know I'm good at that."

Jack and his daughter both laughed at that remark.

&

She and Lucas attended the last football game of the season for Porttown High. They won. Now regionals loomed ahead for the team.

"Thanks for driving, Meredith. I felt really weird asking you out, then asking you to drive. If everything goes OK, I get my driving privilege back after Christmas. I can't wait. I hate riding my stupid bike to the vet for work. You know, you taught me something, what consequences mean. You seem to have picked that up real early. Me, well, what I learn I always learn the hard way. It's my curse."

Meredith looked over to him as she parked her car at the crowded restaurant where everyone met after the game.

"Hey, let's go in and have fun, OK?"

She beamed a big smile to him as they held hands before entering the café. He watched her smile and smiled back to her.

7

Meredith stood back for a moment before she brought more rolls from the kitchen.

"God, thank you, I feel joy, in my heart. These are all dear folks," she prayed.

She looked from Tyler to Colin.

"I love them; I love them both. One will be near me, and one will be far from me," her mind spoke.

Jack and Jess and Hailee, Colin and Laura, Uncle Milt and Conner, she watched them enjoying the meal as she returned to the table. Every diner helped himself to seconds. And everyone asked for their pumpkin pie and whipped cream as soon as they all helped clear the main course dishes. Since the gals did the meal, the guys decided to man up and do the dishes. Colin led the way.

"Come on, guys, I gotta do it all at my house."

He heard no grumbling. The guys knew more pie awaited them.

ॐ

Meredith and Tyler sat close on the couch later that evening.

"Been a really difficult semester for me, Meredith, the leadership of the detachment cadets, and my studies, man oh man, I have a senior projects class that is a bitch, a group study, there are seven of us. I feel like I've sorta been distracted, not really in the swing of what is going on. I got so much on my mind right now."

"The leadership of the cadets, went OK?

She turned to look into his eyes.

"I didn't tell you, but we lost a cadet, icy roads, so we had a memorial in Leadership Lab for her, and then her funeral, in her home town, not far from Manhattan. That was awful, Meredith."

She watched him tear up, shaking his head, "So young, a young light gone out," he said in a shaky voice.

They held each other for a time.

"I care so much, Tyler."

"And I care for you, Meredith, you'll be back soon, and I'll be so glad."

They separated from their hug.

"Hopefully you can relax a bit tomorrow, what do you want to do?"

Tyler shook his head to Meredith. She watched his sad teary eyes.

"What, what?"

"The weather forecast changed. Possible snow is forecast in the Manhattan area on Saturday, want to get back before that weather change." He looked into her eyes, "I'll go tomorrow afternoon."

"You must be safe, Tyler."

He nodded. She watched a small smile come to his lips.

"I love you for that, Meredith, you get it, flying involves risk, especially a little plane. I know that; I know the risk. Thank you."

He cupped his hand under her chin and put light feathery kisses all over her lips and lower face.

Meredith felt her groin fire up, the sexual attraction, her for him; it was real, and powerful.

"How to handle this?" she asked herself.

Tyler took her hand and placed it on his groin. She felt his penis straining against his slacks.

She removed her hand.

She whispered to him, "We desire."

And he replied, "We'll just desire."

They separated their bodies and looked in each other's eyes.

"I wrote you, last summer, that you are my lovely light."

"I remember, Tyler. And you said my light will not be there in the fall."

"It sure wasn't." He directed his gaze to her eyes, "I missed that light. Now there's that light in your eyes, a light like from a star, it'll stay with me, your light will shine on me, 'til you get back to school and we can see each other again."

Meredith smiled, "Not long now, Christmas coming, and then school starting." She paused, "You know what Tyler, I thought about what you said about a light, hey you already got a light. It's a light that shines within you. I got that inner light too."

They sat in the quiet.

Meredith watched Tyler turn his head toward her, "You forgot one date on the calendar."

Meredith looked into his eyes, shaking her head, not understanding.

"Your birthday, Missy, you'll be 17 on the 29th."

"Yeah, I get everything over with in a quick hurry," she giggled. "Once upon a time my folks had an unbirthday day for me in July, a cake and everything, 'cause it was forever until my birthday on top of Christmas."

&

The next morning Meredith and Tyler drove Conner to work. She took Tyler to The Flower Shop to introduce him to Dena. She showed him around and explained how the shop and ordering system operated. He asked about flower arranging. Tyler watched Meredith and Dena as they put together a small arrangement to demonstrate for him.

"Wow, you guys perform like artists, using flower colors instead of paints and clay. Definitely you create wonderful smelling arrangements."

ဢ

The skies looked content, at least in Tyler's eyes after he hugged Meredith and gave her a final kiss.

"Not long now, we'll be together," they nodded and smiled to each other.

Meredith jumped up and down as he turned to her and waved before getting in his plane. Meredith heard the purr of the engine as he taxied down the county airport runway. She put her hand over her eyes as Tyler's plane rose into the sky. She waited, straining her eyes, waiting. She saw it and jumped up and down again. Tyler wiggle waggled the wings of his plane.

"Safe flight, my love," Meredith shouted out.

ဢ

Early in December the Porttown Symphony performed their holiday songs before a packed house. The community looked forward to the start of the holiday season with the Symphony's special music. Colin sat with the Raymer family. He and Laura continued to spend time together. Meredith got no clues as to how their relationship was evolving.

"Besides," she told herself, "it is for sure none of my business. Colin and I still visit once in a while. I am happy with their situation and my part in it."

On the drive back to the ranch Meredith asked the three men about their favorite part of the concert.

"Oh Mere, the lady who told the story of Good King Wenceslaus, you know, with the small chorus humming in the background and the symphony playing the main song, that's my favorite."

"Mine too, Conner," Meredith added.

"How he cared about the cold and starving man outside the castle, how he helped his page by telling him to walk in the King's footsteps, I liked that a lot, he seemed like a kind man, the lady said he went out into the winter and helped folks."

"That's what Christmas is all about, being kind to others, being at peace with one another," Uncle Milt added.

&

"Dad, where's all the stuff for Christmas?"

"Lemme think, Meredith."

Meredith sat across from her dad at the breakfast table the morning after the concert.

She watched him shake his head.

"You headed to K State. You know how we like to keep the tree up and the decorations for a while after Christmas. Your mom wouldn't take down the tree or the other decorations."

Jack looked at his daughter and started tearing up.

"I got a little embarrassed about that. I should'a seen that was the start of her letting go of everything here. One night in late January Conner helped me take down the ornaments and put the tree back in its box. We just dragged everything into the garage. But after your mom left, we started junking up the garage with just plain old garbage. I knew I needed to find a space out in the barn for all the stuff. I don't remember where she used to keep the decorations. But, yeah, now they have a happy home in the barn. Want me to show you?"

"Nah, just point me in the right direction. I'm gonna put up the tree; it's over three and a half weeks until Christmas.

I want our home in order and Christmas stuff down before I leave for school early in January."

Jack smiled to his daughter, "I love you, Meredith, your initiative, take-charge attitude, you're the best. Please decorate. We'll all enjoy whatever you decide to do."

Meredith nodded to him.

"I'm glad to see his eyes are not teary, it's still so hard for him, with mom. It'll be their first Christmas apart for," she paused in her thought, "many years."

"Later, Dad," Meredith rose and walked to her room as tears formed in her eyes, her mind remembering her mom, and Cole.

"I wonder how much longer I'll have these pangs of sadness for those who are no longer with us?"

She grabbed her coat and satchel and headed to work.

℘

That night Meredith found the boxes of Christmas decorations, dusted them off, and brought them to the living room. She unboxed the three sections of the artificial tree and put them together and stood the tree up. Conner helped her decorate the tree with ornaments, some from their childhood. Jeepers sat by, taking in all their activity.

Conner smiled and held up the decoration, "Mere, here's my little train. Remember all the years you and me played with Thomas the Train?"

Meredith came to him and hugged his shoulder, "And all those years we made Lego buildings for around the tree, our Lego Christmas village."

"Fun, right Mere?"

Conner watched her smile to him and then to the tree, "Times I'll never forget, Conner."

"The Nativity scene," she stopped as she held the boxes for the crèche and the other characters.

"Mere, it's the most important part of Christmas."

"So, Conner, where?"

Conner started to clear the coffee table, "Here, OK?"

"Conner, it's another work day for you tomorrow. I'll finish."

"Sure?"

They hugged and Meredith finished setting up the scene as she hummed *Silent Night.* Meredith loved the crèche. She and her mom put it out and talked about the special characters, Mary, Joseph, Jesus. That memory swirled in Meredith's head.

"Mom, I need to wish you a Happy Christmas. Conner and I will call you," Meredith told herself to remember to do that.

ಬ

"I'll need a couple of days to get organized for spring semester."

"So," Dena watched Meredith look at the calendar.

"My last day will be Tuesday before New Year's Day. I'll drive to Manhattan on Saturday. The dorms open up Friday, and classes start on Monday."

"Is your family ready?"

Meredith smiled to Dena and caught her eye with a funky expression on her face, "Yeah, as ready as they'll ever be, you know guys. Least ways mine, don't groove on the old stuff, you know housekeeping, around the house."

Dena started to laugh, catching Meredith up in the laughter too.

"How about the shop?"

"We're all set; I got the raise I wanted. Amber is working out, starting to get goals, like you, 'cept your goals are huge, the degree, the commission."

"Hey, everybody has different goals, different plans for their lives." Meredith paused, and started to nod her head, "We're all God's children, our wings, well, all the same."

ॐ

Christmas Day brought quiet to the Raymer home. On that morning, to the surprise of all of them, including Uncle Milt, they talked about missing Julie, Meredith and Conner's mom, especially after Meredith and Conner opened the gifts their mom mailed to them. She sent them each a picture of her. Meredith fixed hot chocolate for everyone as they sat in their pj's to open presents. Colin came to their noon Christmas meal. Food relieved a sadness and gave better spirits to everyone.

"The ham, it's so perfect," Colin mentioned to the family.

"I picked it out; I know which ham tastes best. I recommend it to our customers at the store," Conner beamed to Colin.

"Good job, Conner."

"Mere, you cooked it up just right, with the spices and the little bit of orange juice poured over it."

"So, what did everyone get for Christmas?" Colin asked.

"New sound system for my room," Conner smiled to everyone.

"Tune up for my car and a new battery," Meredith spoke up.

"Uncle Milt and I asked for a fine corn crop, which we got. That is our best Christmas present."

They watched Uncle Milt and Jack nod their heads.

"Everyone pitched in, and it was wonderful," Jack's eyes shone with appreciation as he looked from Milt to Conner, to Meredith, and then to Colin.

"Again, everyone, thank you for adopting me and helping me with my corn harvest."

Meredith watched Jack nod to Colin, "Hey man, we'll do er again next fall."

"Walk me to my car, OK?" Colin asked Meredith after everyone helped with the dishes and put the leftovers in the fridge. Colin held a piece of pie for a snack at home.

"We demolished the apple and pumpkin pies, right?"

"Yeah, you guys all have big sweet tooths."

Meredith stood next to Colin as they stopped near his truck.

"I love you, Meredith, know that, and that my thoughts are with you as you travel back to Manhattan. I do and will always keep you in my prayers, and I am so grateful for you."

Meredith watched his shining thankful eyes, "And I love you, Colin. You are in my prayers. I know you will let me go from your mind one day."

He nodded to her, "But never from my heart."

Colin watched as instant tears came to Meredith's eyes.

"Here, give this to your dad for the guys, it's a gift certificate to their favorite eating place in town. They're gonna miss your cooking."

Colin kissed her on her forehead and got into his truck and drove out the lane. Meredith gave him a wave, and he waved back.

Meredith went straight to her room after she handed the certificate to her dad. She knelt by her bed, and cried, "God help me go on, to give thanks for all I have."

It took her a few minutes to collect her thoughts and face her family. It was time for a board war game they played every holiday season. And like almost every other year, after four hours of wiping out country after country, Jack won with his usual whoops and shouts. He took over the whole world.

"Dad, master of the universe for another year," Conner teased his dad. Meredith heard hearty laughter go all around.

☙

Meredith liked going to work at the shop the next day. She and Dena transitioned the front-window display to an in-between season, anticipating the upcoming Valentine holiday. Most of all she got to think through her next few weeks, back at State. On Saturday Meredith helped with a holiday wedding. She, Dena, and Amber decided this was the most beautiful time of the year to marry. They did just a little prep work at the church. A lovely tree already graced the sanctuary. The reception, like the wedding, was small. The shop's petite holiday floral arrangements decorated the tables, clothed in green tablecloths. The bridal couple and families liked everything The Flower Shop created for the affair. Dena recommended the caterer to the families. Meredith thought the food tasted scrumptious. The lovely wedding and reception made Meredith feel wonderful, she being a part of a glorious joining of two people.

℃

Meredith's family took her out for her 17th birthday. Conner brought home a carrot cake from the store, decorated with her name on it. They ate cake and ice cream as soon as they got home from their favorite café in town. Meredith opened her cards from Conner, her dad, and Uncle Milt. Everyone respected her wish for no presents.

"Mere, you need to go to your bedroom."

"Conner, why?"

He smiled to her, "Just go."

She opened the door to her room. A spicy odor caught her nose. She turned on the light. Twelve beautiful red roses in a green vase sat on her desk. "So awesome, oh wow," she spoke out as she dipped her nose near the flowers. She breathed in the delicious smell and removed the card settled in among the roses.

She read the card, *Meredith, I love you. We'll be together soon. I know you are ready for this semester, and I wish the best for you, with your classes and with your time in the detachment. Tyler*

Meredith brought the roses out to show her family.

"These belong on the dining room table, for all to enjoy."

Jack came up to her and held her by the shoulder, "From Tyler?"

Meredith gazed into her dad's eyes. She teared up as she nodded her head to him. She removed one rose from the bouquet and took it back to her room after she cut off a lot of the stem. Her bible sat on top of clothes already packed away in her suitcase.

"Tyler, I'll keep this rose in my bible; I'll press it on the page from Ecclesiastes about a time for every season. You and I, we're in the early bloom of our lives, and the rose will remind me of that," she spoke out. Meredith kissed the rose and placed it at Ecclesiastes 3.

ℂ

"I am happy, real happy," Meredith said to her brother and her dad before she and Conner left for work the next morning.

"Soon you'll be where you want to be, Mere," Conner told her in his quiet voice.

"Right, Conner."

She noticed his sad eyes and tried to keep from tearing up.

"Conner, please keep Jeepers with you at night. He was a huge comfort to me. I turn him over to you, OK?"

"Thanks, Mere, he always greets me when I come home, always glad to see me. I like that a lot."

They said their goodbyes to their dad and drove to the grocery store. Meredith let Conner off and headed to the shop. At lunch that day she drove her car to her church and stopped in.

Meredith looked around the darkened room. Dark wood planks pointed up into an A-line roof. The brick walls held stained glass windows, four windows on each side of the room. Comfortable red cushions graced the seats of the dark wood pews. A thick red carpet ran the length of the room, from the entrance to the altar.

"God, I feel your presence, like a soft cloth wrapped gently around me. Guide me this next semester in Manhattan. Keep my family safe here in Porttown and mom in California. I called mom, and she wished me good luck this semester at school. I'm grateful for the experiences I've had since I returned last spring." She paused, "I grew up."

Meredith looked straight ahead at the darkly stained window behind the altar. "You are my strength, now in my time of joy," she whispered.

෨

"Let's say goodbye tonight, Dad. I've already said my goodbye to Conner."

"Well, sweet pea," Jack stopped and gazed into his daughter's eyes as they sat across from each other, having one last cup of coffee together, "thank you for taking time off to help us out. I am, forever," he paused, "grateful."

"Dad, I'm projecting ahead; you will have the care of Conner and Uncle Milt for the rest of your life. Are you sure you'll be OK with that, two special- needs men in your life?"

"Yeah, Meredith, I am. I probably will outlive Milt. Conner is another matter," he shook his head. She saw his eyes gazing ahead, beyond her, thinking. "The docs, when Conner was born, indicated that he might live into his forties, but that was some time ago. He's surpassed everybody's expectations of what a mentally-disabled person can do. He's stayed remarkably thin, exercises because of your example, and he remains healthy. Often times, folks have their hearts give out, with the Down syndrome. And Meredith, I now have a wonderful friend, Jess, she's given me advice, and she's worked with special kids."

Jack reached across the table and rubbed Meredith's upper arm, "We're gonna be OK."

Meredith smiled to her dad; she watched him return her smile with a big one of his own.

8

As Meredith drove out her lane she glanced across the fields on both sides. She saw stubble everywhere, from the corn they harvested in October.

"Soon, dad, you'll be plowing this up and getting ready for another corn crop," she spoke out, "corn, it's another part of our circle of life."

She made it to Manhattan late on Saturday before the storm. Meredith unloaded her car in five loads and parked in the assigned parking lot. Her dorm was newer; she liked the look of the open reception area on the main floor. Her room seemed bigger and nicer than the room she had the spring semester before. She and her roommate communicated several days before Meredith left for school. Meredith gazed around the room she shared with Whitney.

"She's moved in, looks like she's neat and organized like me. That's so good," Meredith nodded as she looked out the window. She watched the wind shaking the bare trees in the yard between the dorm wings. She moved her eyes up to the clouds overhead.

"Snow coming, definitely, but Tyler, you'll make it, you're due in before dark," she spoke out.

❧

Stacey invited Meredith and Travis to her room for snacks and pop later that evening. Stacey and Travis were both cadets in the detachment. And they lived in Meredith's dorm.

Hugs went all around as the three of them met. They sat on the floor in Stacey's room and ate popcorn with their sodas.

"I missed out on all the fall stuff with you guys."

"Fun, hard work, the detachment grows. You know we lost a cadet," Travis said

"I'm so sorry, that's gotta be tough for all of you."

"We didn't know her, a freshman. Tyler did a great job with all of us as cadet leader. Meredith, he's got super leadership abilities; he'll go far 'cause the cadets love him no, respect him, just like we know his enlisted men will care for him when he commands a group as an officer," Stacey smiled to Meredith and Travis and nodded her head.

"You guys know what I have to do; read all the book that you all covered last semester. Thanks, Stacey, for bringing me my copy."

"It's the history part of the Air Force; I love history, so I'm loving the course," Stacey told her.

"Yeah, our officer makes it interesting, so much went on after we got started as an Air Force in 1947," Travis agreed.

❧

Meredith woke to a light snow falling outside her window. She peeked out and saw the dusting of snow on the ground.

"This coffee, uuummm great," Meredith said to Whitney, "not like the weak stuff they served at my last dorm."

They shared Christmas-break experiences as they ate their breakfast.

Meredith drove to church alone that Sunday. She saw the Christmas decorations and the life-size scene of the manger still adorning the inside of the beautiful little church. She remembered during the service about removing all the decorations in her own home before leaving.

"Thank you God," she prayed, "for my knowing I needed to get my home in order. What happens now is out of my control. My family'll be fine. Dad really likes Jess. That may be a match. My family sure could use more happiness. I know they hated to see me go, tears all around about that."

On the way out of church she shook hands with her minister who remembered her from a year ago.

"Welcome back, Meredith," the reverend said to her as she paused for a moment.

"We got the corn crop in," Meredith gave him a wide smile and a thumbs up. She watched his smile and nod of understanding. The light snow started again mid-afternoon after she called her dad and let him know she arrived in good shape. She liked her new dorm, and her new roommate.

"Dad, my books, geeesh, way expensive."

She told him the amount.

"Yeah, books are expensive, sweet pea, but you have your sights set high; it's all good. Have you seen Tyler?"

"Naw, I'm not worried, he's a busy dude, passing on the cadet detachment commander lead to the new cadet leader."

Meredith paused, "I love you, Dad. Please let Conner know I love him, Uncle Milt, too, OK?"

"Consider it done."

∞

Meredith bundled up, getting ready to go to the University library to do some reading. On the way out of her dorm hallway Travis stopped her.

"Meredith, I got a call, s'posed to get with Stacey. Our colonel wants to meet all cadets at the detachment at 1800. It's important, casual, no uniform, got it?"

Meredith smiled to him and nodded. She took three of her texts with her to the library and read for several hours. The dorm dining hall filled up for supper; more students arrived for the start of classes Monday.

"This is sure a luxury, not having to do the cooking," she mentioned to Whitney as they ate.

"So, you were pretty much in charge at home?"

"Right."

Meredith decided to share a little information about herself with Whitney. Whitney told some of her life story. They both had family situations where they had to let go of what happened to other family members. They needed to concentrate on themselves, and what they needed to do for their own futures.

ℳ

Meredith, Stacey and Travis walked to their building a few minutes before 1800. The skies cleared. Stars studded the sky as they looked up and away from the building lights. The cadets and officers jammed into the biggest classroom. Meredith saw cadets she did not recognize, the freshman class. Stacy and Travis looked about and saw four faces, adults as old as the officers, faces they did not recognize.

The colonel raised his hand at 1800. The room quieted. Meredith directed her gaze to him. She watched him scan the room, from left to right, going in a slow deliberate fashion, looking at his cadets. Her stomach started to turn. Her ears held the quiet of the classroom.

"About 1030 today I received a call from our CAP (Civil Air Patrol) commander. Those of you who fly know how closely we work with them."

The colonel nodded his head, and Meredith watched quite a few cadets nod theirs in agreement.

"He informed me of a downed plane a few miles from Middleton, that's half way between here and our eastern border. At 1330 he called back with a confirmation regarding the pilot of the plane. Of course the NTSB (National Transportation and Safety Board) is handling the accident. Our Tyler Calva, the medical examiner at the scene, indicated it's our Tyler."

Screams and crying erupted across the room. Sobs became wails. Meredith heard sounds of despair emanating from cadets. Meredith heard, yet she did not feel. A fog numbed her mind. She remembered it from Cole's death, from her mom's leaving, and from Ginny Ann and the baby dying.

"We're going to break up now."

The colonel assigned an officer and a university counselor to each of the four classes.

"Let's go quickly to your assigned room."

Meredith moved with the sophomore cadets. She looked around, not really seeing anyone, just faces.

"I've never seen this officer before," she shook her head as she watched the man approach the front of the room with a counselor.

"Tyler's in heaven with God," Meredith whispered.

She listened to what the officer and counselor had to say. She heard a vague reference to a snow squall. Some of their words replicated what she heard in her counseling sessions back home.

After 10 minutes cadets who wished to stay and talk to the officer and counselor broke from the rest of the group. All Meredith wanted was to get out of there. She walked back to her dorm alone. She needed to.

"God," she whispered, "it's Your will, not mine. But know this, God, Tyler remains with me, in my heart. His desire to pursue his dream, he was doing that, putting more miles on his plane, getting more expertise in flying. God, he died doing what he loved. I hope that's what happens to me one day, that I die doing what I love, doing my dream."

She got coffee to take to her dorm room. After she cried her heart out, she called her dad. He talked; she cried, then she talked.

"What I wanta know, Dad, why do men who love me die? Am I a curse?"

"Sweet pea, ya know that only God can answer that. Just keep loving, your family, your fellow cadets, invite as much love into your life as you can, now and once this anguish is over."

"Thanks, Dad."

"It'll take a while; give it time, Meredith."

෨

Each night that first week back in classes Meredith found her way to the library from after dinner until 9:30. She walked back to her dorm and studied in the dorm study area until midnight.

"I'm gonna stay caught up in all my classes," she explained to her roommate after three nights of the same study hours.

Meredith sat on her bed and looked across at Whitney who plumped pillows behind her back.

"Girl, please take care of yourself, OK?"

"I will, Whitney, I won't have Saturday to study, 'cause we're carpooling to Lawrence for Tyler's funeral."

"Hey, how're you doing with that?"

"I love him; I miss Tyler, but I will go on. I've my whole life ahead of me. He wanted me to accomplish my dreams. Right now, all I can do is put one foot in front of the other."

෨

Every night Meredith opened her bible to Tyler's rose. She smelled the faint odor of the rose and read the verse. The little exercise helped Meredith sleep at night. Her brain fog came back as she sat through Leadership Lab on Thursday and stood at Tyler's graveside service in Lawrence on Saturday. Most of the sophomores, juniors, and seniors in the detachment attended the service in uniform. Again, Meredith had trouble concentrating on what the minister said during the brief service. She also really didn't hear the comments of her detachment colonel. Instead she watched the sky, searching for a plane, Tyler's plane, a plane she could see so clearly in her mind's eye. She swore she could hear the engine's hum.

"He's with God, he's with God," she spoke to the cadets on either side of her.

The Calva's invited the detachment to their home for food after the service. Meredith heard the music Tyler loved, soft country, some bluegrass, playing as the mass of young people circulated inside and in the backyard of Tyler's home. The cadets consumed large quantities of pizza, sodas and cupcakes.

Meredith took a few moments when his parents were free.

"I'm Meredith," she extended her hand to Tyler's dad.

He shook hands with her and put his other hand over hers.

"He loved you," Roderic Calva spoke, tears in his eyes.

Meredith let go of his hands and came to him with a hug. She felt another set of arms go around her. It was Tyler's mom. They held together, in silence.

"Thank you for coming, Meredith, and for the opportunity to meet you."

Tears ran in rivulets down Meredith's face. All she could do was nod to Tyler's parents. She excused herself and stepped outside the home. She wiped her eyes and nose and took a walk down the street. When she got to the corner, she looked up to the sky. She watched white bouncy clouds moving along against a pale blue sky. Meredith stretched out her arm and raised it up. She searched slowly across the sky with her arm as a pointer, looking for planes, for contrails, for Tyler.

ℰℴ

Colin got the call from Jack Raymer several days after Meredith called her dad.

"She's lost a special person in her life, Colin."

"Yeah, I sure understand. And I know what I need to do for Meredith."

Colin bid his time. He knew Meredith needed to grieve, as he still needed to from time to time. He shared what he knew with his new friend, Laura. She understood too. She lost her mom to breast cancer two years before.

ℰℴ

Chemistry caught Meredith up, its difficulty holding her mind from the agony of losing another loved one. After two weeks of hard work and study Meredith decided to take a Saturday afternoon off. She came back from the library, caught her laundry up and had a leisurely lunch of soup and salad.

She decided to go for a walk around campus, not wanting to get in her car and drive anywhere. On her way out of the reception area she felt strange, a presence that she did not see.

"Meredith, turn around."

It took Meredith a minute to understand, to remember the voice. She turned around and saw a tall figure approaching her.

"Meredith."

At first she didn't recognize him. Her mind began to clear.

"Colin?" she whispered, "is that you?"

Colin watched her eyes, tears coming hard, "Yes, it's me."

Now she saw tears in his eyes. She looked from his handsome face to his extended arm. She accepted the red rosebud from him. They each stepped forward and came into a hug.

"Oh Colin, you came all this way to see me, thank you, oh thank you."

"You are my friend, Meredith," he whispered to her. "It's what friends do."

Colin and Meredith walked for hours. Meredith showed him the entire Kansas State campus. They ate at the Student Center and ended up in front of her detachment building. They stood outside. The sky darkened, and they felt the January chill set into their bones.

"Come here," Colin said as he gathered her in his arms. "I'll keep you warm."

They stayed in the hug for a little while.

"Colin," she said as she stood a little away from him, "that sky, oh all those stars, they're little holes in the floor of heaven."

"Yeah," he said as they both focused their eyes on the sky.

She held his hand, and they turned to the building.

"It's locked, but Colin, lots of dreams and hopes, too, start in this building for my fellow cadets." She turned to him, "Richard Myers was a cadet in this detachment. He had dreams, wanted to be a pilot like Tyler. I miss Tyler so much," she shook her head and looked up into his eyes.

"I know you do." Colin paused, pulling up an old conversation in his mind, "Think you told Cole about Myers before you left for school. Cole told me what you told him, so I looked this Myers up. One man can accomplish a great deal, as he has. You admire him?"

"Right."

Colin put his arm around her shoulder as they walked toward her dorm.

"I'm staying at a motel close to campus. Let's meet for early church and then let's go to brunch, OK? I gotta head down the road after that."

Colin watched her turn her head to him.

"Sounds perfect, Colin. I've had such a grand time with you today and tonight. I'm exhausted; these last few weeks, hell for me."

"My life is good; Laura is good, I see your dad and uncle often. You guys, you're my family now," he smiled as he nodded to Meredith. "Please, I want you to work hard, keep trying, your hopes and dreams," he looked into her eyes, "will continue to unfold."

"I don't want him to go; I want him to stay with me," the tape played round and round in Meredith's head as she held hands with Colin in church and as they ate the delicious brunch. Colin stood next to her by her car in the restaurant parking lot.

"Meredith, you are in my thoughts and prayers, and I love you."

He watched her eyes looking up to him and the smile on her face.

"And I love you, Colin."

They came into a strong hug. Colin's lips descended on hers. They held in that kiss for a very long time.

"Godspeed, Colin," Meredith smiled, her eyes filled with tears.

She watched him nod, get in his car and head east to Iowa. Meredith drove out in the country to think about the past few days. She glanced ahead and out the right side window. A clear blue sky held her gaze. She pulled over and got out. In her hand she carried the red rose, now beginning to open up. Meredith searched the skies, for a plane that might be flying up high. She saw none. She smiled to herself, holding the rose.

"Thank you God, for my life," she shouted up to the sky.

Meredith watched, her eyes following the rose as she pointed it to the sky, from left to right, searching, searching.

She would keep trying, as she always had, as Colin suggested to her, as her future unfolded.

ॐ

Dear Reader,
And what of Meredith? There will be a sequel.

A VOICE FOR GABBY

Almost 15-year-old Gabby survives an explosion which takes the lives of her teammates and her spirit team sponsor. Her brain injury leaves her without memory or the ability to speak. Gabby's dad helps with her educational rehabilitation through the summer after the accident. She decides she will work hard to represent her former team by being a good student.

Her neighbor, Josh, comes back into her life. He and his sister played with Gabby when they were younger. Josh's affection for Gabby grows as he spends time with her. Her parents and Josh support her as she progresses through relearning how to read. She must also review eight years of schooling, for which she has no memory.

Still unable to speak Gabby retakes ninth grade at Hillyer, a school better suited to her educational situation. She discovers she can dance and has gymnastics ability learned over past years. Dancing brings her happiness, and she hopes that somehow she may start to regain other parts of her memory.

Josh and Gabby now attend the same school. Their friendship grows. Gabby discovers sexual feelings in herself and for Josh. Her mom gives her a book explaining what is going on with her body. Gabby does well at Hillyer and begins to feel she is catching up in her studies, except in English. Spelling and writing essays continue to be difficult for her. Her English teacher suggests books she needs to read over the summer before her sophomore year. A part time job and reading books keep her busy. She passes both her written and practical driving exams and becomes a cautious driver.

Josh suffers serious injuries while riding his bike. Gabby spends time with him through his hospitalization and rehabilitation. She loves him, as he loves her. Gabby joins a new spirit team at Hillyer. Dancing brings her joy. While out riding bikes with Josh as part of his rehab, she speaks two words. With speech therapy she begins to regain her voice, from a loud soprano in the past to a soft, scratchy alto now. At the first fall pep assembly she dances with the new spirit team. As she performs, she feels a bright light surrounding her. She remembers again what a miracle she is.

ABOUT CATHLEEN

www.CathleenEllis.com

Cathleen Ellis is a Colorado native. She and her husband, John, live in the northern part of the state. They have four sons, three daughters-in-law, and four grandchildren. Cathleen draws the inspiration for her love stories from the lives of young people with whom she has lived and worked her entire life.